CAST UPON
THE BREAKERS

Horatio Alger, Jr.

CAST UPON THE BREAKERS

FOREWORD BY RALPH D. GARDNER

1974
Doubleday & Company, Inc.
Garden City, New York

ISBN: 0-385-08386-6
Library of Congress Catalog Card Number 73–9003
Foreword Copyright © 1974 by Doubleday & Company, Inc.
All Rights Reserved
Printed in the United States of America
First Edition

CONTENTS

Contents 7

FOREWORD:
THE LAST ALGER HERO!

Rodney Ropes, the champion of *Cast upon the Breakers*, is the last Alger hero. With the publication of this novel—serialized in a nineteenth-century magazine under a pseudonym and unnoticed for over eighty years—all of Horatio Alger's hero fiction is now published. Thus, we culminate an amazing era in American popular literature.

The end of that era began last year with the publication of another long-lost Alger, *Silas Snobden's Office Boy*. Astonishing things happened when *Silas* appeared, the first bona fide new book by the famed author of success stories to appear in sixty-three years.[1] Senior citizens who hadn't read Alger since childhood jubilantly renewed old acquaintance, and many youngsters—some perhaps gently prodded by parent or grandparent—tried and liked it.

Media cordially welcomed this relic by a nineteenth-century writer whose name is an American colloquialism but whose works—like cigar-store Indians or Currier and Ives prints—have more recently reposed in that Valhalla known as Americana. Well in advance of publication, trade journals called it "a delight,"[2] assuring booksellers that "this rattling good tale is gen-yew-ine Alger!"[3] In a feature article stretching seven columns

across the top of a page, the New York *Times* found *Silas*
"filled with startling relevancies."

Critics' praises soon followed. *Time* magazine proclaimed:
"The Age of Aquarius gets an extraordinary first edition"; Associated Press in a national release hailed it as "a publishing
coup," the *Christian Science Monitor* (headlining their review
"Horatio Alger Succeeds Again") considered "this lately discovered treasure . . . the most unusual new novel of the sea-
son." The New York *Times Book Review* reported "a great
deal of the marvelous about it" and *Saturday Review*, calling
Alger "the most popular American storyteller who ever lived,"
added "the book goes down as easily as home made ice cream
. . . complete with the cherry on top." The *Philadelphia Bul-
letin* reviewer simply exclaimed, "What a capital idea!" The
book went into its second edition prior to publication and
showed (albeit toward the bottom) on at least one best seller
list.

The mystery of *Silas*'s delayed resurrection—it had gone un-
detected since it was printed in *The Argosy* late in 1889—was
due primarily to the fact that the story carried a long-forgotten
Alger pseudonym. "Thereby," wrote one reviewer, "somehow
getting lost in the shuffle from serial to book. And therein is
the miracle, not [the] discovery of the mistake, but the mistake
itself, like unearthing a case of Scotch in W. C. Fields's basement."[4]

That pen name—Arthur Lee Putnam—also appeared above
the present novel, similarly concealing its author's true identity
from the time it was serialized three years later in the same pe-
riodical. Using the Putnam by-line seemed reasonable enough
at that time. Actually, it was employed by the wily publisher,
Frank A. Munsey, a dozen times over several years to avoid
confusion with Alger-signed stories that ran concurrently. All
other Putnams, however, eventually appeared as books with
Horatio Alger, Jr., properly credited as the author.

The only advance notice ran the week before its first installment, vouching that "those who have read Mr. Putnam's earlier
serials need not be told that they have a great treat in store in
the perusal of *Cast upon the Breakers*. Suddenly thrown on the
world to make his own way in life, Rodney Ropes develops a
pluck and courage that cannot fail to inspire admiration and a
strong desire to follow his fortunes as he leaves school to battle
for his daily bread."[5]

Thus are we introduced to Rodney Ropes, the Last Alger
Hero. His adventure brings to a final tally of 109[6] the long list
of such sturdy, alliteratively named companions as Ben Bruce,
Tom Temple, Dean Dunham and Ned Newton, all of whom
led devotees of generations past through action-packed pages of
books titled *Do and Dare, Fame and Fortune, Frank and Fearless, Luck and Pluck, Risen from the Ranks* and *Rough and
Ready*.

But Alger's efforts were not limited to hero fiction. Like Sir
Arthur Conan Doyle, who in addition to the Sherlock Holmes
stories produced historical romances, political pamphlets and
notable writings on spiritualism and the occult, and Charles
Dodgson, whose *Alice* classics (written under the pseudonym
Lewis Carroll) overshadowed mathematical treatises and poetic
works, Horatio Alger—a New-England-born, Harvard-educated
teacher and minister[7]—produced poetry and short stories plus a
number of attempts at adult literature. To complicate biblio-
graphical examination of his output further, he took a variety of
pen names, two books were published anonymously and after
his death in 1899 his name appeared as author of eleven juven-
iles which were, in fact, written by the prodigious Edward
Stratemeyer. Still later, F. Scott Fitzgerald borrowed an Alger
title for an Alger-like story of his own creation.[8]

Alger's first book, *Bertha's Christmas Vision*—a collection of
twenty early short stories reprinted from various weekly and
monthly story papers—appeared in 1856. The next year he is-

sued *Nothing to Do*, a slim volume of poetry, followed by five novels that attracted little attention. It was Alger's eighth book, *Ragged Dick*, issued in 1868, that catapulted him to best-seller-dom—a position his works maintained throughout his lifetime and well into the 1920s—originating the formula for the series of tales he churned out at the rate of three or four each year.

Although *Cast upon the Breakers* assuredly is the last in which an Alger hero meets adversity head on, scatters the enemy and comes out farther on top than ever before, there still remain two of his novel-length stories which never were issued as books. These are *Marie Bertrand*, issued in 1864 in Street & Smith's *New York Weekly*, and *A Fancy of Hers*, printed in *Munsey's Magazine*, March 1892.[9] Both were for adults, but with the unmistakable Alger touch. Marie Bertrand eked out a scanty living as a seamstress in Paris before discovering, in the closing lines, that she was really the kidnapped daughter of the Baroness de Conray. *A Fancy of Hers* also had a heroine. She was Mabel Frost Fairfax, a prominent New York society girl who, fed up with the social whirl, applied incognito for a teaching job in a New Hampshire hamlet. The story was advertised as "The strange experiment of a New York girl—A village romance and a series of sketches of village types."

Two of Horatio Alger's books also featured female protagonists,[10] but his forte was the honest, incredibly good-humored, hard-working teen-age lad in patched pants who—through quick thinking and incredible luck—foils assorted street corner toughs; upstages sniveling, cane-twirling snobs; outsmarts burglars, jewel thieves, railroad con men, embezzlers by the dozen and kidnappers; performs daring, heroic rescues (old folks and children were his specialty)—all the while improving his education, prospects and bank balance.

From Civil War days almost until our Great Depression, kids bought, swapped and borrowed every Alger thriller that came off the presses. Parents approved, ministers recommended them and, judging from teachers' presentation inscriptions, Algers led all the rest as prizes for penmanship, punctuality and Sunday school excellence. It is safe to assume that, during this era of America's transcontinental expansion, industrial growth and the arrival of wave upon wave of immigrants from distant lands, virtually every boy and many girls read Alger. Those who grew up to prominence often credited these easily digestible tales as having wielded good influence. Unquestionably, Alger's name has become a synonym for rapid rise from humble beginnings to sparkling success. And Alger's hero is, more so today than ever before, as legendary as Parson Weems' fable of George Washington and the cherry tree, the prowess of Davy Crockett or Abraham Lincoln's cracker barrel wisdom.

Alger's style of fast-paced dialogue, non-stop action and invariable happy ending have always provided a bonanza of fun and inspiration for his admirers; they are anathema to his detractors. One of the latter, Brooks Atkinson, the respected former drama critic of the New York *Times*, described Alger as a "prodigious hack," and a "literary mechanic." Nevertheless, he admitted, "there is no doubt that he was a huge commercial success. Every man who was a boy before World War I must have read some of these tales of success achieved through virtue and industry." Why, wondered Atkinson, couldn't Alger write like Dickens, "who was making literature out of the miseries of London by writing with gusto, outrage and humor"? Supposing Alger was "everybody's good uncle," he suggests that "if he was fabulously successful, it must have been because he wrote sincerely"; that his stories "express his personal philosophy." Concluding, Atkinson termed Alger "a bachelor of life and letters whose nonsense in his mature years suited the nonsense of thousands of boys many years ago."

It was upon my then recently published biography of Horatio Alger that Brooks Atkinson was commenting. Although I remained silent, others did not. Several weeks later he devoted

another *Times* column to this subject. "Some disparaging re-
marks here about the literary eminence of Horatio Alger Jr.
have not delighted the nation," he began. "Too many adults
have fond memories of *Phil the Fiddler* and *Ragged Dick*."

One Staten Islander recalled that he never thought of Alger as
literature, but "just plain enjoyed the Alger books. I was like a
little boy with a warm puppy," he says. "They made me feel
comfortable, safe, secure." A Virginian suggested that no harm
would be done if today's "youngsters were exposed to these
same inspiring stories," and a New Yorker who "came to America in 1913, at the age of nine" wrote: "I learned the language
quickly and as rapidly was exposed to Alger, first in newsboys'
clubs and then in that underestimated treasure-house, the Public Library of New York. I read all the Alger books and then
went on to Optic, Altsheler on the Civil War, and Henty with
the English and Scott with the Scottish backgrounds; and
from them to Dickens, Twain and Poe, etc." This writer declared "that Alger's attitudes toward hard work and tenacity
and Alger's standards of propriety and ethical conduct permanently shaped his belief in America as a land of opportunity."[11]

Regrettably, too few of Horatio Alger's modern carpers have
recently, if ever, read one of his stories, for they too often use
all-embracing, inaccurate and misleading platitudes. Three
most recurrent are that the Alger hero was too good to be true;
that he inevitably became a millionaire; and that he always
married the boss's daughter. Had they but joined those who
cavil "If you've read one, you've read them all" (which also is
not completely true), or "All they ever cared about was making
money" or "None of them ever rescued a *poor* man's child!"
they might find some modicum of textual support.

Alger's manly young chaps *were* courteous, considerate to
their elders and widowed mothers, but the author tried hard to
avoid crowning them with a halo. Rather than risk them being

judged angelic, he added flaws to their character. Ragged Dick, when introduced as a homeless bootblack, gambled, squandered two cents for shots of whiskey, spent evenings at the ill-reputed Old Bowery Theatre and enjoyed penny cigars. Tom the Bootblack confessed he had been drunk and Mark the Match Boy had a fondness for cigarettes. The hero of *Tom Temple's Career* was known as the bully of the village, and Jack Harding, in *Jack's Ward*, played unconscionable pranks upon an old maid aunt. Needless to say, all reformed.

Occasionally, Alger spiced narratives with conversation morsels that, although familiar to newsboys and baggage smashers, seemed wickedly raunchy to his disciples. Ragged Dick, whose dwelling was an empty barrel in an alleyway off the Bowery, took on all comers in fistic or verbal duel. He sassed the neighborhood ruffian or drop-game swindler with finesse. But he excelled at humiliating the snobbish fop.

One morning on Lower Broadway, "only a few blocks distant from the Astor House," Dick was addressed by "a rather supercilious-looking young gentleman, genteely dressed, and evidently having a very high opinion of himself." He "turned suddenly to Dick, and remarked,—

" 'I've seen you before.'

" 'Oh, have you?' said Dick, whirling around; 'then p'r'aps you'd like to see me behind.' "

Tattered Tom, who was a girl, was even rougher!

There is not a single instance in Horatio Alger's output of any hero becoming a millionaire. Rather than fabled riches, they sought to pay off the mortgage on the old homestead and achieve middle-class respectability. Although their bright futures were forecast, Paul the Peddler merely graduated from street salesman of nickel prize packages to necktie vendor to shopkeeper. Near the conclusion to *Sink or Swim*, Harry Raymond—having "seen something of the world"—returns to his village just in time to save his mother's mortgaged home and thwart Squire Turner's treacherous schemes.

"Foiled at all points," Alger gleefully reported, Turner "dashed his hat angrily upon his head and rushed from the house in undignified haste . . . Harry, who is now twenty-one, is about to take charge of the New York office of Lindsay & Co., which will give him a commanding business position." In *Frank and Fearless*, Jasper Kent rescued little Harry Fitch, who had been kidnapped. The boy's father, in appreciation, rewarded Jasper with a job in his countinghouse. Chester Rand, coming into possession of five lots of land in Tacoma, Washington, shrewdly sold three "for eight thousand dollars, half cash and the balance on a year's time at twelve percent interest." Chester kept one thousand, investing three in several "low priced city lots." Before long he had spun off the remaining two original properties for five thousand dollars each and could unload the others at substantial profit, but preferred to hold them as an investment.

Ragged Dick was lounging at the rail of an East River ferry when six-year-old Johnny Rockwell "fell over into the water."

"At the child's scream, the father looked up, and, with a cry of horror, sprang to the edge of the boat. He would have plunged in, but being unable to swim, would only have endangered his life, without being able to save his child.

"'My child!' he exclaimed in anguish,—'Who will save my child? A thousand—ten thousand dollars to anyone who will save him!'"

Dick, an expert swimmer, dove to the rescue, emerging soaking wet but with a fine career predicted in the grateful Mr. Rockwell's office. However, with customary forgetfulness, Alger never confirmed whether Dick got the cash.

When heroes stepped from curbside to office or store, they started at weekly salaries of four or five dollars. But when getting the job was in appreciation for brave services rendered, it was as much as ten dollars—a substantial sum in those days—and the lad, although still not wealthy, had made an important leap up the ladder.[12]

I cannot think of any Alger tale in which the hero marries. Alger knew nothing of romance and preferred to omit it. He projected such events into the future and prophesied—as he did in *Sink or Swim*—that "there are rumors that Maud, whose early preference for [Harry Raymond] still continues, will, before very long, become the wife of her father's young American representative."

There was no romance because, while these stalwarts stood up to bullies, they were—much like the author himself—awkwardly timid when face to face with the opposite sex. Contacts were most often with older women, from tyrannical wives of poorhouse overseers, shrewish stepmothers and Hogarthian rumpots to careworn mothers, helpful neighbors and generous benefactresses. This group he could cope with. But bright, winsome little girls—whom Alger called "mischievous," "high-spirited," "flirtatious" and "teasing"—were another matter.

These fascinating creatures were daughters of employers and benefactors and, at first sight, impishly announced to Daddy that they were setting their caps for his handsome office boy. They invited the bashful hero to their homes for tea and he suffered dancing lessons to acquit himself satisfactorily at their parties. But when they addressed him, he fumbled for words; when they flattered him, he blushed.

In his typically unsophisticated manner, Alger tried his best to create a romantic milieu for *Sink or Swim*.

Harry Raymond was off digging for gold in Australia. Thirteen-year-old Maud Lindsay—"attractive, lovable, warm-hearted and impulsive"—is telling her father, a wealthy English merchant, that she wishes Harry would return.

" 'It's so lonesome since he went away,' she said.

" 'I begin to think you are in love with Harry, Maud.'

" 'I begin to think so too, papa. Would you object to him for a son-in-law?'

" 'Just at present I might. I don't think you are old enough to be married.'

" 'Don't be foolish, papa. Of course I don't want to be married till I am old enough . . . If I don't marry Harry Raymond, I'll be an old maid.'

"Indeed, Maud had hardly ceased speaking when a knock was heard at the door. Maud rose to open it. She was overwhelmed with delight when, in the visitor, in spite of his rough garb, she recognized our hero, the loss of whose company she had been deploring.

" 'O Harry, how glad I am to see you!' she exclaimed, actually hugging Harry in her delight. Harry was rather embarrassed at the unexpected warmth of his reception, but felt it would be impolite not to kiss Maud in return, and accordingly did so."

This was the only romantic kiss recorded by Horatio Alger in more than one hundred novels![13]

The period Alger portrayed seems to us a golden age of determined youths striving to become successful men through vigor and ingenuity. Rustic scenes exuded a sweet verdancy, while the cobbled streets of Lower Broadway, crowded with hurrying throngs, clattering wagons, pushcarts and carriages, gave off a certain jolly hum as Horatio Alger's newsboys, bootblacks and American District Telegraph messengers struggled to survive and win in a tough game. They lived in "a dream world in which a nightmare is gradually transformed into a sweet dream of success."[14]

Wouldn't it be interesting, then, if Horatio Alger returned today to relate his hustling heroes to a nation almost a century older than the one he knew; to defend the Work Ethic he preached? What would he tell cynics who now poke fun at his exhortation to

> *Strive and Succeed!* The world's temptations flee;
>   Be *Brave and Bold!* and *Strong and Steady* be!
> Go *Slow and Sure,* and prosper then you must;
>   Win *Fame and Fortune* while you *Try and Trust!*[15]

Might he find a boy like Carl Crawford who, in *The Odds Against Him,* labored in a furniture factory for two dollars a week; like Luke Larkin who, in *Struggling Upward,* received "a dollar a week for taking care of the schoolhouse," and earned as much more doing odd jobs around his village? Who, like the enterprising Grit, *The Young Boatman,* today invests his total savings of a few dollars to buy a skiff and rows passengers a half mile across the Kennebec River for ten cents ("but if it were a child or poor person" Grit did it for five)? And who, like Harry Walton, the farm lad of *Bound to Rise,* becomes a cobbler's pegger at three dollars a week after a period of apprenticeship?

It would not be easy to find many youngsters in present-day America who are cheerfully ready to accept those terms. Even if one applied, he would be hindered by dozens of ordinances from earning his livelihood as Alger's boys did. In addition to minimum wage and hour legislation, he would have to contend with compulsory education statutes, city, state and federal labor acts, workmen's compensation, a variety of income taxes, Social Security, medical and other insurance deductions, prerequisites for union membership (with dues deducted), full-time and vacation working permits, street trades licensing fees, indoor and outdoor employment regulations, business zoning restrictions, public contracts laws and probably a number of others that he could be violating.

Thus, Paul the Peddler would be handed a summons at his

street corner and, most likely, Tom the Bootblack, Ben the Luggage Boy and Dan the Newsboy would, at very least, be told to keep moving if a policeman happened along.[16]

It might also be interesting to learn Alger's reaction to a nation's indebtedness to modern Squire Turners through charge accounts, credit cards, layaway plans, buy now-pay later, installment buying, low-cost borrowing, bank loans to pay off other debts, etc.

Reading Alger today is to leap across some great divide and blissfully roll back the light-years to a more tranquil, less complicated time and place he loved and described as no other American author has ever done. And for this uncounted millions of readers adored him! Although without a fraction of Dickens' literary ability, Alger shared Dickens' affection for his world and characters (Horatio could not even hate his villains!) as well as his social indignation.[17] Always percolating a kind of festivity, Alger again and again presented a sound case for the American Dream. And his influence was phenomenal!

In his accounts of the New England countryside, readers could almost hear the rattle of milk pails on the farms and taste the low-bush blueberries that grew large as grapes on sunny hillsides. But it was in his Baedeker-like descriptions of Manhattan that a sort of lyricism came through, despite a technique of writing that may have seemed stilted and archaic even to his Victorian audience.

Horatio Alger briefly visited New York during the Civil War, moving there permanently in the early spring of 1866. Virtually all the stories written during the remaining thirty-three years of his life had as their focal point city sidewalks, with a great deal happening among shabby tenements, by the fenced borders of City Hall Park, within inexpensive Bleecker Street boarding-houses and genteel brownstones situated on and near Fifth Avenue.

His heroes slept (for six cents a night) at the Newsboys'

Lodging House and readers consumed with expectant delight their encounters in Bowery saloons and pawnshops, in Wall Street, at Barnum's Museum, the Astor House and Fifth Avenue Hotel, and their eventful rides on ferries that crossed the East River to Brooklyn.

In the course of his day's work and sometimes in pursuit of thieves or other evildoers—whom Alger liked to depict as "intemperate"—the hero hurried onto a Broadway stage or elevated railroad. One had to concentrate to shut out sounds of the hooves of giant dray teams pulling their loads through noisy, narrow streets, and the shouts of hawkers, shrill above the drone of crowds and traffic. But one mile uptown Alger showed the way to hushed, dignified Washington Square, where children played on the green under the watchful eyes of nursemaids.

Horatio Alger loved his adopted city and exhibited it in a variety of ways. Frequently, the story's hero was hired to guide an out-of-town traveler. This afforded the opportunity to board the horsecars and point out newspaper offices surrounding Park Row, A. T. Stewart's department store, Cooper Institute, Grace Church, Tiffany's and other fine Union Square emporiums. The hero never displayed New York's squalid backwaters to visitors but Alger, nevertheless, escorted readers through the infamous Old Brewery district, Mulberry Bend, The Five Points and Seventh Avenue, "which possessed an unenviable notoriety as the promenade of gangs of ruffianly men and boys whose delight it is to attack and rob peaceable wayfarers."[18]

In a style unlike anything being written today and which, even in its own time, stood volumes ahead of any competition, Alger always gave his lads time to rest on a bench at Madison Square Park. Exuberantly, he displayed aristocratic mansions on Madison Avenue where the boy delivered a message, returned a lost gem or wallet or worked evenings as companion to a benefactor's child.

On mild Sunday afternoons, the hero enjoyed pastoral delights of "the" Central Park, strolling past The Mall, through The Glen or Sheep Meadow. He had, the author would explain, indulged himself to the extent of ten cents, the stage fare from The Battery to Forty-second Street, the car-line terminus. From there he walked northward to the park entrance at Fifty-ninth Street. The sun always shone brightly on those clear spring days of long ago, and Horatio Alger called attention to marble-fronted Fifth Avenue palaces passed en route.

Alger's early books were written when the park itself was still unfinished. No residences of good appearance enhanced it at that time, architecture being limited to goat-herding squatters' huts and temporary sheds used by park laborers.

"The time will undoubtedly come," he accurately predicted, "when the Park will be surrounded by elegant homes and compare favorably in this respect with the most attractive parts of any city in the world." But at the moment, he declared, "not much could be said either of the Park or its neighborhood."

Turning homeward at dusk, our hero made his way back along Sixth Avenue, his outing then highlighted by refreshment at an ice cream parlor. If the weather had turned brisk, he chose, instead, a large bowl of steaming oyster stew.[19]

Publisher Frank A. Munsey took paternal pride in *The Argosy*, its authors, new features, contests; and its growing circulation and popularity. In editorial page comments, he expressed elation over "ten years of triumphal progress," vowing "stronger stories than ever before," and announcing that his "treasure laden magazine," formerly available only by subscription, would "now be found every Saturday on news stands throughout the Union."

Although he had recently moved his editorial offices uptown from Warren Street to the impressively more prestigious and higher rent environs of East Twenty-third Street, he nevertheless reduced rates for the larger format, fourteen-page weekly. Henceforth, it would cost five cents a copy at newsstands, with subscriptions "two dollars per year, payable in advance," or at "three dollars for two years, it costs less than three cents a week."

At these prices he offered the top-notch talents of Alger, Putnam, Edward Stratemeyer, Arthur M. Winfield (a Stratemeyer pseudonym), Annie Ashmore, W. Bert Foster, Oliver Optic, Matthew White, Jr., and a vast army of other crafters of spine-tingling tales. Each issue, Munsey promised, will be brimful of suspense narratives, "every one of which is as crisp as a new ribbon." Captivating titles included *The Cruise of the Dandy*, *A Publisher at Fifteen*, *The Lone Island; or, Adventures Among the Savages*, *A Desperate Chance* and *The Markham Mystery*.

There were instructional articles on raising homing pigeons, dog training, swimming and trout fishing. Timely reports concerned Lieutenant Peary's new polar expedition ("to make a fresh attempt to wrest its secrets from the frozen Northland"); the coming America's Cup Race ("Lord Dunraven has nominated his Valkyrie. British pluck is proverbial. This year she shall try once more"); arrival of the circus ("ten acres at least are required to put up the tents. To transport Barnum & Bailey's aggregation of attractions from town to town, sixty-four cars are employed"); and Chicago's Columbian Exposition ("to commemorate the discovery of our country, is the grandest, the most complete, the most beautiful creation of the kind that has ever been held on earth . . . For instance, the great Madison Square Garden in New York could be dropped inside its Manufacturers and Liberal Arts Building, with acres of space to spare"—later, however, Munsey was "horrified by the fearful prices one had to pay for food to sustain the inner man while the outer feasted on the sights").

The publisher dispensed opinions, advice or warnings on a

variety of current topics: "A good many young people who had been content to run before," he noted, "are now mounted on bicycles with the power to fly like the wind. There are frequent complaints of reckless riding and indifference to the rights of pedestrians on the part of wheelmen." He returned to this problem some weeks later, serving notice that "kyphosis bicyclistarum, the stoop affected by so many wheelmen" could be the fate of those "who do not sit up straight so that they can keep a good lookout ahead."

Alert to needs of urban ecology, Munsey approved of having "pupils of New York City public schools instructed by their teachers in the love of cleanliness, and then sent forth as missionaries to work a reform in front of their own doorsteps. Should the space before each house be swept and garnished, the whole town would be a miracle of neatness." Apprehensive that tall structures would turn city streets into shadowy canyons, he wrote: "It may not be generally known that there is a law in all our large cities regulating the height of buildings. In New York the height shall not exceed eighty feet; in Chicago the recently adopted maximum height is 130 feet and in Boston it is 125 feet for all buildings except the spires of churches."

As summer approached, Munsey wondered about the "freakish fun of bathing among ocean breakers that burst over a man's head, or his being picked up by a wave and thrown down with a slam on the beach. Then," he added, "there is the roller coaster, an undeniably dangerous device for shooting pleasure seekers down a decline at breakneck speed."

He lamented the near extinction of the buffalo. "There are so few that only three figures are needed to reckon up their number." He cited "Buffalo Bill and his kind, with English 'sportsmen' and American army officers who vie with each other in the wanton slaughter of these shaggy headed beasts, once the monarchs of the American plains."

Munsey was a former Maine farm boy who considered himself to be a kind of Alger hero and admired others who achieved prominence. Regularly, he urged readers to emulate the accomplishments of such a diverse group of distinguished figures as Antonín Dvořák, "the son of a butcher in Bohemia whose salary as director of the National Conservatory of Music is $15,000 per year"; Adolph Sutro, mining genius of the Comstock Lode, "one of the multi-millionaires of San Francisco, of whom we hear so much in the East"; the philanthropic Baron Maurice de Hirsch, "whose daring and sudden rise to affluence recall the Monte Cristo of fiction"; and Thomas A. Edison, who, as a Detroit newsboy of fifteen in 1862, bought on credit one thousand copies of the *Free Press* containing reports of the Battle of Pittsburg Landing, selling them at countryside railroad stops for twenty-five cents a copy. He "finished the day with $250 in his pocket, representing several hundred percent clear profit."[20]

Except for the fact that Alger heroes never bought on credit, Rodney Ropes combined the acumen of a young Tom Edison with the ambition and guts of others so highly esteemed by publisher Munsey. His story began in *The Argosy* issue dated Saturday, May 27, 1893, continuing through thirteen installments and concluding August 19. It carried the Arthur Lee Putnam pseudonym because *Victor Vane; or, The Young Secretary*, which properly named the prolific Alger as author, was appearing in the same issues.

Cast upon the Breakers is a narrative in perpetual motion. It is unique in that it combines the variety of basic plot elements that Alger customarily wove into at least two or three separate tales. These include a boarding school episode, a train derailment followed by a robbery and an exciting chase, a score of haps and mishaps on the streets of New York, a coastal voyage to Boston on "the Puritan, the magnificent steamer of the Fall River Line" and the old Vermont homestead saved. Finally,

there is an added bonus of mettlesome exploits beyond the
Great Plains in Montana gold mine country.

This novel runs the crime gamut more intensively than most
Algers, beginning with an embezzled inheritance, then swiftly
proceeding to such an array of archvillainy as jewel robbery,
theft of merchandise, false accusation, swindle, perjury, kidnap-
ping and ransom. But it is the author's familiar hallmarks that
give *Cast upon the Breakers* dramatic surprise and, perhaps, its
hugest dividend of charm. These comprise lovingly detailed descriptions of rural types recalled from his own childhood, his
New York settings and spirited continuity of dazzling episodes
which, although masterpieces of naïveté, nevertheless produced
a tremendous impact upon millions of readers.

Substituting the village of Burton, Vermont, for Chelsea or
Marlborough, Massachusetts, where Alger was raised, he de-
votes amiable attention to Hector, the driver of "an old fashioned Concord stage [that] connected Burton with the railway"; Frank Dobson, a young carpenter who loaned his friend
"a hundred dollars, which was about all the money he had
saved up"; the aged farmer Cyrus Hooper and his wife, Nancy,
who are about to lose their mortgaged property to Squire
Lemuel Sheldon, who "puts on the airs of a millionaire" and
plots a profitable resale of Hooper's land to railroad developers.

There always was much personal biography in Alger's books,
especially those in which the New England countryside and its
inhabitants are viewed in graphic detail. The author frequently
assigned to characters the personalities—occasionally even the
names—of persons remembered from his youth. There is little
doubt, for instance, that crafty village squires were based upon
the mortgage holder of his own father's bankrupt farm. The
family had lived impecuniously on the country parson's meager
income and it is his father whom—as the minister, Canfield—
Alger portrays in *Cast upon the Breakers* as "the man who baptized me when I was an infant. The good old man has been

preaching thirty or forty years on a salary of four hundred dollars and has had to run a small farm to make both ends meet."

The delineation of Rev. Canfield provides an accurate picture of Rev. Horatio Alger, Sr.: "He was venerable looking, for his hair was quite white, although he was only sixty five years old. But worldly cares which had come upon him from the difficulty of getting along on his scanty salary had whitened his hair and deepened the wrinkles on his kindly face."

Alger gathered notes for his Montana chapters during the summer of 1890 while visiting a former pupil, Alfred Lincoln Seligman, who had settled at Helena to manage family mining interests.[21] But it always was the adventures set amid vividly described scenes of Manhattan that his audience fervently anticipated. New Yorkers sensed a pleasure of personal involvement in these chronicles. Those who lived far from the big city devoured them in joyous awe.

Cast upon the Breakers, appearing for the first time as a book more than eighty years after it was written, presents Horatio Alger in peak form. For old-timers who ages ago relished his simple tales of courage and honesty triumphant, a happy excursion into nostalgia is assured. For younger readers who have only heard of Horatio Alger, Rodney Ropes—the Last Alger Hero—now opens wide the gates to a wonderful new world.

Read on! Read on!

Ralph D. Gardner

New York

1. Horatio Alger, Jr., Foreword by Ralph D. Gardner, *Silas Snobden's Office Boy* (Garden City, N.Y.: Doubleday & Company, Inc., 1973). The story's only previous publication was as a thirteen-part serial in *The Argosy*, November 30, 1889–February 22, 1890.

2. *Publishers Weekly*, December 18, 1972, and *Library Journal*, February 1, 1973.

3. *The Kirkus Reviews*, December 15, 1972.

4. John Seelye in "A Sanctuary of Male Innocence," New York *Times Book Review*, March 25, 1973.

5. *The Argosy*, May 20, 1893, p. 176.

6. *Silas Snobden's Office Boy*, op. cit., p. 6 and footnote 2, p. 25; also, Ralph D. Gardner, *Road to Success; The Bibliography of the Works of Horatio Alger* (Mendota, Ill.: Wayside Press, 1971), p. 14.

7. Horatio Alger, Jr., was born at Chelsea (now Revere), Massachusetts, January 13, 1832. He was a member of the Harvard class of 1852, being elected to Phi Beta Kappa and graduating eighth in a class of eighty-eight. See Arthur M. Alger, *Memorial of the Descendants of Thomas Alger, 1665–1875* (Boston: Press of David Clapp & Son, 1876), pp. 15, 28, 45 et pas.; also, Benjamin Shurtleff, *The History of the Town of Revere* (Boston: Beckler Press, Inc., 1938), pp. 120, 150, 276–77, et pas.; also, Grace Williamson Edes, *Annals of the Harvard Class of 1852* (Cambridge: The University Press, 1922), pp. 54, 121, 193, 332, et pas. Alger began a teaching career while an undergraduate, continuing after graduation and, still later, serving as tutor in the classics to a number of prominent New York families. See *Silas Snobden's Office Boy*, op. cit., footnote 4, pp. 25–

26; also, Ralph D. Gardner, *Horatio Alger; or, The American Hero Era* (Mendota, Ill.: Wayside Press, 1964), pp. 118, 121, 124, 200, et pas. Alger attended the Cambridge Divinity School, finishing July 1860, later serving as pastor of the First Parish Unitarian Church of Brewster, on Cape Cod. Alger resigned in March 1866, after being accused of a homosexual incident by a church-appointed committee. See Richard M. Huber, *The American Idea of Success* (New York: McGraw-Hill, 1971), p. 45; also, *1866 Records of the First Parish Unitarian Church*, Brewster, Mass. Alger then moved to New York, pursuing a full-time career as a writer. For many years he made the Newsboys' Lodging House his headquarters. Professor John Seelye, of the University of Connecticut, in the *New York Times Book Review*, op. cit., states: "If Alger had indeed been an active homosexual, he would have been as a fox among chickens, but the very fact of his presence in the home for so many years suggests that, whatever his inclinations, he restrained them. Instead, proximity bred perceptiveness —Alger knew what boys wanted from a book better than most children's writers, then and now." Horatio died at South Natick, Massachusetts, July 18, 1899.

8. Alger's two anonymous works were *Nothing to Do; A Tilt at our Best Society* (Boston: James French & Co., 1857), and *Timothy Crump's Ward; or, The New Year's Loan, And what Came of it* (Boston: Loring, Publisher, 1866). In addition to the Putnam pseudonym, Alger is known to have used Arthur Hamilton at least twice and Julian Starr once. In addition, the pen name Caroline F. Preston was frequently signed to short stories on which Alger collaborated with his sister, Olive Augusta Cheney. Starting within a year after Alger's death, eleven novels appeared which, although they carried the name of Horatio Alger, Jr., as author, were actually written by Edward Stratemeyer, who styled himself as "Alger's literary executor." Although Stratemeyer—who became a fabulously successful editor and author—claimed these were completions of works Alger left unfinished at the time of his death, they appear to be 100 per cent Stratemeyer, without a trace of Alger. See *Road to Success*, op. cit., pp. 21, 25, 96, 120, et pas.; also, Quentin Reynolds, *The Fiction Factory; or, From Pulp Row to Quality Street* (New York: Random House, 1955), pp. 83, 117; also, unsigned article about Stratemeyer, "For It Was Indeed Him," *Fortune*, April 1934, pp. 86–89, 193, 204, et pas. F. Scott Fitzgerald's Alger-influenced story, for which he even adopted Alger's title, *Forging Ahead*, appeared in 1929 in the *Saturday Evening Post*. The tale's seventeen-year-old hero, Basil Duke Lee, took a job in the Great Northern Railway car shops to earn money to pay his way through Yale.

9. *Road to Success*, op. cit., pp. 67, 90, 91.

10. *Ibid.* The two novels with female protagonists were *Helen Ford* (Boston: Loring, Publisher, 1866), and *Tattered Tom* (Boston, Loring, Publisher, 1871). *Helen Ford* was Alger's only attempt at fiction for girls. His heroine is a young singer, the sole support of her unworldly father, an inventor who is trying to build an airplane. The author doesn't believe this can be done, commenting: "No man of a well balanced mind would have labored with such sanguine expectations of success on a project so uncertain as the invention of a flying machine." At story's end, Alger advises: "Mr. Ford has long since given up his invention as impractical" (pp. 79–80). Readers were often surprised to learn that Tattered Tom—one of Alger's roughest characters—was a girl. Nevertheless, this is one of the most typical of his works, and certainly one of his most popular. Like Marie Bertrand, Tom had been kidnapped in infancy from a wealthy home (pp. 119–20).

11. Brooks Atkinson, *Brief Chronicles* (New York: Coward-McCann, Inc., 1966), pp. 180–82, 185–97. The column, "Prodigious Hack," originally appeared in "Critic at Large," New York *Times,* July 24, 1964. "The Flaw in the Alger Formula" appeared September 18, 1964. Regrettably, in the latter column Mr. Atkinson quotes an often repeated hoax "that Alger, after being graduated from Harvard College, embraced the wickedness of women with scandalous abandon and annoyed the wits out of a married woman whom he haunted in New York and Paris when he was in his sixties. 'I can't get rid of him,' she wrote to her brother helplessly. 'If the passion were momentary I would not mind it; but he repeats and repeats his intention of staying near me. What am I to do?'" This fiction was created by Herbert R. Mayes in *Alger: A Biography Without a Hero* (New York: Macy-Masius, 1928). For many years, doubting scholars have questioned and refuted the Mayes version (see *Silas Snobden's Office Boy,* op. cit., p. 6 and footnote 3, p. 25). Mr. Mayes, a retired magazine editor and publisher, is especially eager to set the record straight. In a letter to Bill Henderson, Associate Editor, Doubleday & Company, he wrote on July 3, 1972: "Not merely was my Alger biography partly fictional, it was practically *all* fictional . . . The project was undertaken with malice aforethought—a take-off on the debunking biographies that were quite popular in the 20's, and a more miserable, maudlin piece of claptrap would be hard to imagine . . . Unfortunately—how unfortunately! —the book when it appeared was accepted pretty much as gospel. Why it was not recognized for what it was supposed to be baffled the publisher (George Macy) and me . . . In any event, the reviewers . . . treated the book as an authentic effort . . . I think Frank Adams considered it a bore . . . One critic . . . accused me of being without imagination. *That* I loved." Writing again on July 12, regarding "internal contradictions" in

his book, Mr. Mayes stated: "Far from denying they exist, I'd guess the book literally swarms with them, along with countless absurdities." My own copy of his book he autographed to me thus: "For Ralph Gardner, with good wishes, from the perpetrator of the hoax. Herb Mayes."

12. *Horatio Alger; or, The American Hero Era,* op. cit., pp. 311, 322, 334, 342, et pas.; also, Michael Zuckerman, Professor of History, University of Pennsylvania, in "The Nursery Tales of Horatio Alger," *American Quarterly,* May 1972, pp. 191–209, says: "The Alger stories were never about the fabulous few who rose from poverty to great riches; they were, at best, tales of a much more accessible ascent from rags to respectability. His nonpareils do not wax wealthy so much as they grow reputable, leaving the promiscuity of the streets for the propriety of a desk job . . . There is not a robber baron in the bunch, nor even a remarkable fortune . . . His aims were social and moral more than they were economic."

13. Bill Henderson in "A Few Words About Horatio Alger, Jr.," *Publishers Weekly,* April 25, 1973, pp. 32–33, wrote: "Horatio spiced his novels with every type of sin except the sexual variety, of which, using his novels as a guide, he knew nothing."

14. John Seelye, in the New York *Times Book Review,* op. cit.

15. Composed of six of his book titles, this was one of Alger's two favorite inscriptions in autograph albums. In earlier versions his third line read: "*Shift for Yourself,* and prosper then you must." The true book title was *Shifting for Himself,* which may account for his eventual switch to "Go *Slow and Sure* . . ." The other rhyme, which has been noted also in presentation copies of his books and appears to have been preferred by him in later years, is the last stanza of his often reprinted poem, "Carving a Name":

> If I would have my name endure,
>   I'll write it in the hearts of men
> In characters of living light
>   From kindly deeds and actions wrought,
> And these, beyond the reach of time,
>   Shall live, immortal as my thought.

16. *Horatio Alger; or, The American Hero Era,* op. cit., pp. 344–45.

17. In *Phil the Fiddler; or, The Story of a Young Street Musician* (Boston: Loring, Publisher, 1872), Alger exposed the cruel, unlawful padrone sys-

tem. This fact-based story described how boys and girls were taken (sometimes bought) from their impoverished homes in southern Italy, their parents deceived that they were being taken to America to receive an education and earn money with which other family members would migrate to the United States. Once arrived in New York and other major cities, these children were sent out on the streets as beggars or musicians. They were trained as pickpockets and thieves. Subjected to inhuman treatment by severe taskmasters, many died. Although citizens and politicians agreed this was outrageous, until Horatio Alger seized the initiative, official policy was to keep hands off and look the other way. It took Alger but six months after his book's publication to doom this criminal traffic. His life was threatened; he was mauled by irate padrones. But Alger stuck to his guns and won. The book provided needed stimulus, forcing the New York State Legislature to pass the first laws preventing cruelty to children. *Julius; or, The Street Boy Out West* (Boston: Loring, Publisher, 1874) was Alger's second powerful social document. The book, using records of The Children's Aid Society, drummed up considerable public support for the organization's project to take hundreds of homeless waifs off city streets and transport them halfway across the continent, where their new foster families were establishing homes along the recently opened western frontier. Later, Alger became interested in the Fresh Air Fund, sponsored by his friend, Whitelaw Reid, owner of the New York *Tribune*. The author pledged wholehearted efforts to this program that arranged country vacations for slum children. In numerous of his works, Horatio Alger protested against child labor conditions as well as those under which women were working as seamstresses for as little as twenty-five cents a day.

18. *Silas Snobden's Office Boy*, op. cit., p. 42.

19. *Horatio Alger; or, The American Hero Era*, op. cit., pp. 327–29.

20. *The Argosy* (New York: Frank A. Munsey & Company, 1893), Vol. XVI, February 25 to August 19, 1893, pp. 190, 204, 246, 273, 288, 308, 315, 358, et pas.

21. *Horatio Alger; or, The American Hero Era*, op. cit., pp. 204, 284.

CAST UPON
THE BREAKERS

CHAPTER I.
A FAITHLESS GUARDIAN.

"Well, good by, Rodney! I leave school tomorrow. I am going to learn a trade."

"I am sorry to part with you, David. Couldn't you stay another term?"

"No: my uncle says I must be earning my living, and I have a chance to learn the carpenter's trade."

"Where are you going?"

"To Duffield, some twenty miles away. I wish I were in your shoes. You have no money cares, and can go on quietly and complete your education."

"I don't know how I am situated, David. I only know that my guardian pays my expenses at this boarding school."

"Yes, you are a star boarder, and have the nicest room in the institution. I am only a poor day scholar. Still I feel thankful that I have been allowed to remain as long as I have. Who is your guardian?"

"A Mr. Benjamin Fielding, of New York."

"Is he a business man?"

"I believe so."

"Do you know how much you will inherit when you come of age?" asked David, after a short pause.

"I haven't an idea."

"It seems to me your guardian ought to have told you."

"I scarcely know my guardian. Five years ago I spent a week at his home. I don't remember much about it except that he lives in a handsome house, and has plenty of servants. Since then, as you know, I have passed most of my time here, except that in the summer I was allowed to board at the Catskills or any country place I might select."

"Yes, and I remember one year you took me with you and paid all my expenses. I shall never forget your kindness, and how much I enjoyed that summer."

Rodney Ropes smiled, and his smile made his usually grave face look very attractive.

"My dear David," he said, "it was all selfishness on my part. I knew I should enjoy myself much better with a companion."

"You may call that selfishness, Rodney, but it is a kind of selfishness that makes me your devoted friend. How long do you think you shall remain at school?"

"I don't know. My guardian has never told me his plans for me. I wish he would."

"I shall miss you, Rodney, but we will correspond, won't we?"

"Surely. You know I shall always feel interested in you and your welfare."

David was a plain boy of humble parentage, and would probably be a hard working mechanic. In fact he looking for nothing better.

But Rodney Ropes looked to be of genteel blood, and had the air of one who had been brought up a gentleman. But different as they were in social position the two boys had always been devoted friends.

The boarding school of which Rodney was, as his friend expressed himself, a star pupil, was situated about fifty miles from the city of New York. It was under the charge of Dr. Sampson, a tall, thin man of fair scholarship, keenly alive to his own interests, who showed partiality for his richer pupils, and whenever he had occasion to censure bore most heavily upon boys like David Hull, who was poor.

Rodney occupied alone the finest room in the school. There was a great contrast between his comfortable quarters and the extremely plain dormitories occupied by less favored pupils.

In the case of some boys the favoritism of the teacher would have led them to put on airs, and made them unpopular with their school fellows. But Rodney had too noble a nature to be influenced by such considerations. He enjoyed his comfortable room, but treated his school fellows with a frank cordiality that made him a general favorite.

After David left his room Rodney sat down to prepare a lesson in Cicero, when he was interrupted by the entrance through the half open door of a younger boy.

"Rodney," he said, "the doctor would like to see you in his office."

"Very well, Brauner, I will go down at once."

He put aside his book and went down to the office of Dr. Sampson on the first floor.

The doctor was sitting at his desk. He turned slightly as Rodney entered.

"Take a seat, Ropes," he said curtly.

His tone was so different from his usual cordiality that Rodney was somewhat surprised.

"Am I in disgrace?" he asked himself. "Dr. Sampson doesn't seem as friendly as usual."

After a brief interval Dr. Sampson wheeled round in his office chair.

"I have a letter for you from your guardian, Ropes," he said. "Here it is. Do me the favor to read it here."

With some wonder Rodney took the letter and read as follows:

DEAR RODNEY—I have bad news to communicate. As you know, I was left by your father in charge of you and your fortune. I have never told you the amount, but I will say now that it was about fifty thousand dollars. Until two years since I kept it intact, but then began a series of reverses in which my own fortune was swallowed up. In the hope of relieving myself I regret to say that I was tempted to use your money. That went also, and now of the whole sum there remains but enough to pay the balance of your school bills, leaving you penniless. How much I regret this I cannot tell you. I shall leave New York at once. I do not care at present to say where I shall go, but I shall try to make good the loss, and eventually restore to you your lost fortune. I may be successful or I may not. I shall do my best, and I hope in time to have better news to communicate.

One thing I am glad to say. I have a casket containing your mother's jewels. These are intact. I shall send you the casket by express, knowing that you will wish to keep them out of regard for your mother's memory. In case you are reduced to the necessity of pawning or selling them, I am sure that your mother, could she be consulted, would advise you to do so. This would be better than to have you suffer from want.

There is nothing further for me to write except to repeat my regrets, and renew my promise to make up your lost fortune if I shall ever to able to do so.

                    Your Guardian,
                  BENJAMIN FIELDING.

Rodney read this like one dazed. In an instant he was reduced from the position of a favorite of fortune to a needy boy, with his living to make.

He could not help recalling what had passed between his friend David and himself earlier in the day. Now he was as poor as David—poorer, in fact, for David had a chance to learn a trade that would yield him a living, while he was utterly without resources, except in having an unusually good education.

"Well," said Dr. Sampson, "have you read your letter?"

"Yes, sir."

"Your guardian wrote to me also. This is his letter," and he placed the brief epistle in Rodney's hands.

DR. SAMPSON—I have written my ward, Rodney Ropes, an important letter which he will show you. The news which it contains will make it necessary for him to leave school. I inclose a check for one hundred and twenty five dollars. Keep whatever is due you, and give him the balance.

BENJAMIN FIELDING.

"I have read the letter, but I don't know what it means," said Dr. Sampson. "Can you throw any light upon it?"

"Here is my letter, doctor. You can read it for yourself."

Dr. Sampson's face changed as he read Rodney's letter. It changed and hardened, and his expression became quite different from that to which Rodney had been accustomed.

"This is a bad business, Ropes," said the doctor in a hard tone.

He had always said Rodney before.

"Yes, sir."

"That was a handsome fortune which your father left you."

"Yes, sir. I never knew before how much it amounted to."

"You only learn when you have lost it. Mr. Fielding has treated you shamefully."

"Yes, sir, I suppose he has, but he says he will try to make it up to me in the future."

"Pish! that is all humbug. Even if he is favored by fortune you will never get back a cent."

"I think I shall, sir."

"You are young. You do not know the iniquities of business men. I do."

"I prefer to hope for the best."

"Just as you please."

"Have you anything more to say to me?"

"Only that I will figure up your account and see how much money is to come to you out of the check your guardian has sent. You can stay here till Monday; then you will find it best to make new arrangements."

"Very well, sir."

Rodney left the room, realizing that Dr. Sampson's feelings had been changed by his pupil's reverse of fortune.

It was the way of the world, but it was not a pleasant way, and Rodney felt depressed.

CHAPTER II.
THE CASKET OF JEWELS.

It was not till the latter part of the afternoon that the casket arrived. Rodney was occupied with a recitation, and it was only in the evening that he got an opportunity to open it. There was a pearl necklace, very handsome, a pair of bracelets, two gold chains, some minor articles of jewelry and a gold ring.

A locket attracted Rodney's notice, and he opened it. It contained the pictures of his father and mother.

His father he could barely remember, his mother died before he was old enough to have her image impressed upon his memory. He examined the locket, and his heart was saddened. He felt how different his life would have been had his parents lived.

He had never before realized the sorrow of being alone in the world. Misfortune had come upon him, and so far as he knew he had not a friend. Even Dr. Sampson, who had been paid so much money on his account, and who had always professed so great friendship for him, had turned cold.

As he was standing with the locket in his hand there was a knock at the door.

"Come in!" he called out.

The door opened and a stout, coarse looking boy, dressed in an expensive manner, entered.

"Good evening, John," said Rodney, but not cordially.

Next to himself, John Bundy, who was the son of a wealthy saloon keeper in the city of New York, had been a favorite with Dr. Sampson.

If there was anything Dr. Sampson bowed down to and respected it was wealth, and Mr. Bundy, senior, was reputed to be worth a considerable fortune.

In Rodney's mood John Bundy was about the last person whom he wanted to see.

"Ha!" said John, espying the open casket, "where did you get all that jewelry?"

"It contains my mother's jewels," said Rodney gravely.

"You never showed it to me before."

"I never **had** it before. It came to me by express this afternoon."

"It must be worth a good pile of money," said John, his eyes gleaming with cupidity.

"I suppose it is."

"Have you any idea what it is worth?"

"I have no thought about it."

"What are you going to do with it? It won't be of use to you, especially the diamond earrings," he added, with a coarse laugh.

"No," answered Rodney shortly.

"My eyes, wouldn't my mother like to own all this jewelry. She's fond of ornaments, but pa won't buy them for her."

Rodney did not answer.

"I say, Ropes, I mustn't forget my errand. Will you do me a favor?"

"What is it?"

"Lend me five dollars till the first of next month. My allowance comes due then. Now I haven't but a quarter left."

"What makes you apply to me, Bundy?"

"Because you always have money. I don't suppose you are worth as much as my father, but you have more money for yourself than I have."

"I have had, perhaps, but I haven't now."

"Why, what's up? What has happened?"

"I have lost my fortune."

John whistled. This was his way of expressing amazement.

"Why, what have you been doing? How could you lose your fortune?"

"My guardian has lost it for me. That amounts to the same thing."

"When did you hear that?"

"This morning."

"Is that true? Are you really a poor boy?"

"Yes."

John Bundy was astonished, but on the whole he was not saddened. In the estimation of the school Rodney had always ranked higher than he, and been looked upon as the star pupil in point of wealth.

Now that he was dethroned John himself would take his place. This would be gratifying, though just at present, and till the beginning of the next month, he would be distressed for ready money.

"Well, that's a stunner!" he said. "How do you feel about it? Shall you stay in school?"

"No; I can't afford it. I must get to work."

"Isn't there anything left—not a cent?"

"There may be a few dollars."

"And then," said Bundy with a sudden thought, "there is this casket of jewelry. You can sell it for a good deal of money."

"I don't mean to sell it."

"Then you're a fool; that's all I've got to say."

"I don't suppose you will understand my feeling in the

matter, but these articles belonged to my mother. They are all I have to remind me of her. I do not mean to sell them unless it is absolutely necessary."

"I would sell them quicker'n a wink," said Bundy. "What's the good of keeping them?"

"We won't discuss the matter," said Rodney coldly.

"Do you mind my telling the other boys about your losing your money?"

"No; it will be known tomorrow at any rate; there is no advantage in concealing it."

A heavy step was heard outside. It stopped before the door.

"I must be getting," said Bundy, "or I'll get into trouble."

It was against the rule at the school for boys to make calls upon each other in the evening unless permission were given.

John Bundy opened the door suddenly, and to his dismay found himself facing the rigid figure of Dr. Sampson, the principal.

"How do you happen to be here, Bundy?" asked the doctor sternly.

"Please, sir, I was sympathizing with Ropes on his losing his money," said Bundy with ready wit.

"Very well! I will excuse you this time."

"I'm awful sorry for you, Ropes," said Bundy effusively.

"Thank you," responded Rodney.

"You can go now," said the principal. "I have a little business with Master Ropes."

"All right, sir. Good night."

"Good night."

"Won't you sit down, Dr. Sampson?" said Rodney politely, and he took the casket from the chair.

"Yes, I wish to have five minutes' conversation with you. So these are the jewels, are they?"

"Yes, sir."

"They seem to be quite valuable," went on the doctor,

lifting the pearl necklace and poising it in his fingers. "It will be well for you to have them appraised by a jeweler."

"It would, sir, if I wished to sell them, but I mean to keep them as they are."

"I would hardly advise it. You will need the money. Probably you do not know how near penniless you are."

"No, sir; I don't know."

"Your guardian, as you are aware, sent me a check for one hundred and twenty five dollars. I have figured up how much of this sum is due to me, and I find it to be one hundred and thirteen dollars and thirty seven cents."

"Yes, sir," said Rodney indifferently.

"This leaves for you only eleven dollars and sixty three cents. You follow me, do you not?"

"Yes, sir."

"Have you any money saved up from your allowance?"

"A few dollars only, sir."

"Ahem! that is a pity. You will need all you can raise. But of course you did not anticipate what has occurred?"

"No, sir."

"I will throw off the thirty seven cents," said the principal magnanimously, "and give you back twelve dollars."

"I would rather pay you the whole amount of your bill," said Rodney.

"Ahem! Well perhaps that would be more business-like. So you don't wish to part with any of the jewelry, Ropes?"

"No, sir."

"I thought, perhaps, by way of helping you, I would take the earrings, and perhaps the necklace, off your hands and present them to Mrs. Sampson."

Rodney shuddered with aversion at the idea of these precious articles, which had once belonged to his mother, being transferred to the stout and coarse featured consort of the principal.

"I think I would rather keep them," he replied.

"Oh well, just as you please," said Dr. Sampson with a shade of disappointment for he had no idea of paying more than half what the articles were worth. "If the time comes when you wish to dispose of them let me know."

Rodney nodded, but did not answer in words.

"Of course, Ropes," went on the doctor in a perfunctory way, "I am very sorry for you. I shall miss you, and, if I could afford it, I would tell you to stay without charge. But I am a poor man."

"Yes," said Rodney hastily, "I understand. I thank you for your words but would not under any circumstances accept such a favor at your hands."

"I am afraid you are proud, Ropes. Pride is—ahem—a wrong feeling."

"Perhaps so, Dr. Sampson, but I wish to earn my own living without being indebted to any one."

"Perhaps you are right, Ropes. I dare say I should feel so myself. When do you propose leaving us?"

"Some time tomorrow, sir."

"I shall feel sad to have you go. You have been here so long that you seem to me like a son. But we must submit to the dispensations of Providence—" and Dr. Sampson blew a vigorous blast upon his red silk handkerchief. "I will give you the balance due in the morning."

"Very well, sir."

Rodney was glad to be left alone. He had no faith in Dr. Sampson's sympathy. The doctor had the reputation of being worth from thirty to forty thousand dollars, and his assumption of being a poor man Rodney knew to be a sham.

He went to bed early, for tomorrow was to be the beginning of a new life for him.

CHAPTER III.
A STRANGE DISAPPEARANCE.

When it was generally known in the school that Rodney was to leave because he had lost his property much sympathy was felt and expressed for him.

Though he had received more than ordinary attention from the principal on account of his pecuniary position and expectations, this had not impaired his popularity. He never put on any airs and was on as cordial relations with the poorest student as with the richest.

"I'm awfully sorry you're going, Rodney," said more than one. "Is it really true that you have lost your property?"

"Yes, it is true."

"Do you feel bad about it?"

"I feel sorry, but not discouraged."

"I say, Rodney," said Ernest Rayner, in a low voice, calling Rodney aside, "are you very short of money?"

"I haven't much left, Ernest."

"Because I received five dollars last week as a birthday present. I haven't spent any of it. You can have it as well as not."

Rodney was much moved. "My dear Ernest," he said, putting his arm caressingly around the neck of the smaller boy, "you are a true friend. I won't forget your generous offer, though I don't need to accept it."

"But are you sure you have money enough?" asked Ernest.

"Yes, I have enough for the present. By the time I need more I shall have earned it."

There was one boy, already introduced, John Bundy, who did not share in the general feeling of sympathy for Rodney. This was John Bundy.

He felt that Rodney's departure would leave him the star pupil and give him the chief social position in school. As to scholarship he was not ambitious to stand high in that.

"I say, Ropes," he said complacently, "I'm to have your room after you're gone."

"I congratulate you," returned Rodney. "It is an excellent room."

"Yes, I s'pose it'll make you feel bad. Where are you going?"

"I hope you will enjoy it as much as I have done."

"Oh yes, I guess there's no doubt of that. I'm going to get pa to send me some nice pictures to hang on the wall. When you come back here on a visit you'll see how nice it looks."

"I think it will be a good while before I come here on a visit."

"Yes. I s'pose it'll make you feel bad. Where are you going?"

"To the City of New York."

"You'll have to live in a small hall bedroom there."

"Why will I?"

"Because you are poor, and it costs a good deal of money to live in New York. It'll be a great come down."

"It will indeed, but if I can earn enough to support me in plain style I won't complain. I suppose you'll call and see me when you come to New York?"

"Perhaps so, if you don't live in a tenement house. Pa objects to my going to tenement houses. There's no knowing what disease there may be in them."

"It is well to be prudent," said Rodney, smiling.

It did not trouble him much to think he was not likely to receive a call from his quondan schoolmate.

"Here is the balance of your money, Ropes," said Dr. Sampson, drawing a small roll of bills from his pocket, later in the day. "I am quite willing to give you the odd thirty seven cents."

"Thank you, doctor, but I shan't need it."

"You are poorly provided. Now I would pay you a good sum for some of your mother's jewelry, as I told you last evening."

"Thank you," said Rodney hastily, "but I don't care to sell at present."

"Let me know when you are ready to dispose of the necklace."

Here the depot carriage appeared in the street outside and Rodney with his gripsack in one hand and the precious casket in the other, climbed to a seat beside the driver.

His trunk he left behind, promising to send for it when he had found a new boarding place.

There was a chorus of good byes. Rodney waved his handkerchief in general farewell, and the carriage started for the depot.

"Be you goin' for good?" asked Joel, the driver, who knew Rodney well and felt friendly to him.

"Yes, Joel."

"It's kind of sudden, isn't it?"

"Yes."

"What makes you go?"

"Bad news, Joel."

"Be any of your folks dead?"

"It is not death. I haven't any 'folks.' I'm alone in the world. It's because I've lost my property and am too poor to remain in school."

"That's too bad," said the driver in a tone of sympathy. "Where are you goin'?"

"To the city."

"Are you goin' to work?"

"Yes, I shall have to."

"If you was a little older you might get a chance to drive a street car, but I s'pose you're too young."

"Yes, I don't think they would take me."

"I've thought sometimes I should like such a chance myself," said Joel. "I've got tired of the country. I should like to live in the city where there's theaters, and shows, and such like. Do you know what the drivers on street cars get?"

"No, I never heard."

"I wish you'd find out and let me know. You can send the letter to Joel Phipps, Groveton. Then find out if it's easy to get such a chance."

"I will. I shall be glad to oblige you."

"You always was obligin', Rodney. I've asked Jack Bundy to do it—you know his folks live in the city—but he never would. He's a mighty disagreeable boy. He never liked you."

"Didn't he?"

"No, I surmise he was jealous of you. He used to say you put on so many airs it made him sick."

"I don't think any of the other boys would say that."

"No, but they could say it of him. Do you think his father is rich?"

"I have always heard that he was."

"I hope he's better about paying his debts than Jack. I lent him twenty five cents a year ago and I never could get it back."

The distance from the school to the station was a mile. Joel fetched the carriage round with a sweep and then jumped off, opened the door, and then helped the passengers to disembark, if that word is allowable.

"How soon does the train start, Joel?" asked Rodney.

"In about five minutes."

"Then I had better purchase my ticket without delay."

"Don't forget to ask about horse car drivers!"

"No, I won't. I should like to have you come to New York. I know no one there, and I should feel glad to see a familiar face."

The train came up in time, and Rodney was one of half a dozen passengers who entered the cars.

He obtained a place next to a stout man dressed in a pepper and salt suit.

"Is this seat engaged?" asked Rodney.

"Yes—to you," and his fellow passenger laughed.

Rodney laughed too, for he saw that the remark was meant to be jocose.

He put his gripsack on the floor at his feet, but held the casket in his lap. He did not like to run any risk with that.

"Are you a drummer?" asked the stout man, with a glance at the casket.

"No, sir."

"I thought you might be, and that *that* might contain your samples."

"No, sir. That is private property."

He had thought of telling what it contained, but checked himself. He knew nothing of his companion, and was not sure how far it might be safe to trust a stranger.

"I used to be a drummer myself—in the jewelry line—" continued his companion, "and I carried a box just like that."

"Ah, indeed! Then you are not in that business now?"

"No, I got tired of it. I deal in quite a different article now."

"Indeed?"

"Suburban lots."

"You don't happen to have any of them with you?"

The stout man roared with laughter, giving Rodney the impression that he had said a very witty thing.

"That's a good one," he remarked, "the best I've heard for a long time. No, I haven't any of the lots with me, but I've got a circular. Just cast your eye over that," and he drew a large and showy prospectus from his pocket.

"If you should be looking for a good investment," he continued, "you can't do any better than buy a lot at Morton Park. It is only eighteen miles from the city and is rapidly building up. You can buy lots on easy installments, and I will myself pick one out for you that is almost sure to double in value in a year or two."

"Thank you," said Rodney, "but I shall have to invest my money, if I get any, in a different way."

"As what, for instance?"

"In board and lodging."

"Good. That is even more necessary than real estate."

"How long have you been in the business, sir?"

"About six months."

"And how does it pay?"

"Very well, if you know how to talk."

"I should think you might do well, then."

"Thank you. I appreciate the compliment. What business are you going into, that is, if you are going to the city?"

"I am going to the city, but I have no idea yet what I shall do."

"Perhaps you may like to become an agent for our lots. I shall be ready to employ you as sub agent if you feel disposed."

"Thank you, sir. If you will give me your card, I may call upon you."

The short man drew from his card case a business card. It bore the name

ADIN WOODS.
ROYAL BUILDING. NASSAU ST.
Morton Park Lots.

"Come to see me at any time," he said, "and we will talk the matter over."

Here the train boy came along and Rodney bought a copy of *Puck*, while the agent resumed the perusal of a copy of a magazine. For an hour the cars ran smoothly. Then there was a sudden shock causing all the passengers to start to their feet.

"We're off the track!" shouted an excitable person in front of Rodney.

The instinct of self preservation is perhaps stronger than any other. Rodney and his seat mate both jumped to their feet and hurried to the door of the car, not knowing what was in store for them.

But fortunately the train had not been going rapidly. It was approaching a station and was "slowing up." So, though it had really run off the track, there was not likely to be any injury to the passengers.

"We are safe," said Adin Woods. "The only harm done is the delay. I hope that won't be long. Suppose we go back to our seats."

They returned to the seat which they had jointly occupied. Then Rodney made an alarming discovery. "My casket!" he exclaimed. "Where is it?"

"What did you do with it?"

"Left it on the seat."

"It may have fallen to the floor."

Rodney searched for it in feverish excitement, but his search was vain. *The casket had disappeared!*

CHAPTER IV.
IN PURSUIT OF A THIEF.

"Were the contents of the casket valuable?" asked the land agent.

"Yes; it contained my mother's jewels, all the more valuable because she is dead," replied Rodney.

"Were they of much intrinsic worth?"

"They must be worth several hundred dollars at least."

"Then they must be found," said Adin Woods energetically. "They have evidently been taken by some passenger during the five minutes we were away from our seats."

"Were you inquiring about the casket?" asked a lady sitting opposite.

"Yes, madam. Can you give any information about it?"

"Just after you left your seat the man that sat behind you rose and reaching over for it went to the rear end of the car and got out."

"I wish you had stopped him, madam."

"He was so cool about it that I thought he might be a friend of the young gentleman."

"I didn't know him. He must have been a thief."

"What was his appearance, madam?" asked the lot agent.

"He was a thin, dark complexioned man, with side whiskers coming half way down his cheeks."

"And you say he got out of the rear end of the car?"

"Yes, sir."

"He won't get on the train again," said the agent turning to Rodney. "He thinks the casket valuable enough to pay him for the interruption of his journey."

"What shall I do then?" asked Rodney, feeling helpless and at a loss which way to turn.

"Follow him," said the agent briefly. "He will probably stop over in the village a day and resume his journey tomorrow."

"Even if I found him I am afraid I shouldn't know how to deal with him."

"Then I'll tell you what I'll do. I'll stop over with you and help you make it hot for him. I've had a spite against thieves ever since I had a valuable overcoat stolen in one of my journeys."

"I shall feel very much obliged to you, Mr. Woods, but won't it interfere with your business?"

"Not materially. If we succeed in overhauling the rascal I shall feel sufficiently repaid for the small interruption. But come on, we can't afford to linger here while he is carrying off the plunder."

"I don't know how I can repay you, Mr. Woods," said Rodney gratefully.

"You can buy a lot of me when you get rich enough."

"I will certainly do so, though I am afraid it will be a long time first."

"You don't know what good fortune may be in store for you. Did you notice, madam, in which direction the thief went?"

"Yes, I was looking out of the window. He went over the road to the left."

"That leads to the village. You will see, Mr. Ropes, that I was right about his plans."

"Don't call me Mr. Ropes. Call me Rodney."

"I will. It don't seem natural to dub a boy Mr. Now, Rodney, follow me."

The two passengers set out on the road that led to the village. They could see the latter easily, for it was not more than a mile away.

"He will be surprised to think we have 'struck his trail' so quick," said the agent.

"Where shall we go first?"

"To the hotel if there is one."

"The village seems small."

"Yes, there are only a few hundred inhabitants probably. It is not a place where a traveler would be likely to interrupt his journey unless he had a special object in doing so, like our dishonest friend. However, I think we shall be able to balk his little game."

Ten minutes' walk brought them to the village. Looking about they saw a small hotel just across the way from a neat white chapel.

"Follow me," said the agent.

They went into the public room in which there was a small office.

The book of arrivals was open, and Adin Woods went forward and examined it. Silently he pointed to a name evidently just written, for the ink was scarcely dry. This was the name: Louis Wheeler, Philadelphia.

"This may or may not be his real name," said Mr. Woods in a low voice.

"Do you wish to register, gentlemen?" asked the clerk.

"We will take dinner, and if we decide to stay will register later. By the way, I recognize this name, but it may not be the man I suppose."

"Yes, the gentleman just registered."

"Would you mind describing him?"

"He was a tall, dark man as near as I can remember."

"And he carried a small casket in his hand?"

"Yes, and a gripsack."

"Oh yes," said the agent, his face lighting up with satisfaction. "It is the man I mean—where is he now?"

"In his room."

"Did he say how long he intended to stay?"

"No, sir. He said nothing about his plans."

"Did he seem specially careful about the casket?"

"Yes, sir. He carried that in his hands, but let the servant carry up the gripsack."

"My friend," said the agent in an impressive tone, "I am going to surprise you."

The country clerk looked all curiosity.

"Is it about Mr. Wheeler?" he asked.

"Yes, the man is a thief. He stole the casket, which contains valuable jewelry, from my young friend here. We are here to demand a return of the property or to arrest him. Is there a policeman within call?"

"I can summon a constable."

"Do so, but don't breathe a word of what I have told you."

The clerk called a boy in from the street and gave him instructions in a low voice. He went at once on his errand, and in ten minutes a stout, broad shouldered man made his appearance.

"This gentleman sent for you, Mr. Barlow," said the clerk.

"What can I do for you?" asked the constable.

"Help me to recover stolen property."

"That I will do with pleasure if you will tell me what you want me to do."

Adin Woods held a brief conference with the constable,

then he led the way up stairs, followed immediately by Rodney, while the constable kept a little behind.

"His room is No. 9," said the bell boy.

The agent paused before the door of No. 9, and knocked.

"Come in!" said a voice.

The agent opened the door, and entered, accompanied by Rodney. A glance showed that the occupant answered the description given by the lady in the car.

Louis Wheeler changed color, for he recognized both the agent and Rodney.

"What is your business?" he asked in a tone which he tried to make indifferent.

"That," answered Woods, pointing to the jewel casket on the bureau.

It looked to him as if Wheeler, if that was his name, had been trying to open it.

"I don't understand."

"Then I will try to make things clear to you. You have, doubtless by accident," he emphasized the last word, "taken from the car a casket belonging to my young friend here."

"You are mistaken, sir," said Wheeler with brazen hardihood. "That casket belongs to me."

"Indeed. What does it contain?"

"I fail to see how that is any of your business," returned Wheeler, determined, if possible, to bluff off his visitors.

"I admire your cheek, sir. I really do. But I am too old a traveler to be taken in by such tricks. I propose to have that casket."

"Well, sir, you are the most impudent thief and burglar I ever met. You break into a gentleman's room, and undertake to carry off his private property. Unless you go out at once, I will have you arrested."

"That you can do very readily, for I have an officer within call."

Louis Wheeler changed color. He began to see that the situation was getting serious.

"There is a great mistake here," he said.

"I agree with you."

The agent went to the door, and called "Constable Barlow."

The constable promptly presented himself.

"Do you want me, sir?" he asked.

"That depends on this gentleman here. If he will peacefully restore to my young friend here yonder jewel casket, I am willing to let him go. Otherwise—" and he glanced at Wheeler significantly.

"Perhaps I have made a mistake," admitted the thief. "I had a casket exactly like this. Possibly I have taken the wrong one."

"I have the key to the casket here," said Rodney, "and I can tell you without opening it what it contains."

"What did yours contain?" asked the agent.

"Jewelry," answered Wheeler shortly.

"What articles?"

"Never mind. I am inclined to think this casket belongs to the boy."

"Rodney, you can take it, and Mr. Wheeler will probably find his where he left it."

No objection was made, and the discomfited thief was left a prey to mortification and disappointment.

Rodney handed a dollar to the constable which that worthy official received with thanks, and he and the agent resumed their journey by an afternoon train. They saw nothing further of Louis Wheeler who sent for dinner to be served in his room.

CHAPTER V.
A YOUNG FINANCIAL WRECK.

"You have been very fortunate in recovering your jewels," said the agent.

"I owe it to you," replied Rodney gratefully.

"Well, perhaps so. If I have rendered you a service I am very glad."

"And I am very glad to have found so good a friend. I hope you will let me pay for your ticket to New York."

"It won't be necessary. The interruption of our journey won't invalidate the tickets we have."

An hour later they reached New York.

"What are your plans, Rodney?" asked Adin Woods, who by this time had become quite intimate with his young companion.

"I shall call on my guardian, and perhaps he may give me some advice as to what I do. Where would you advise me to go—to a hotel?"

"No; it will be too expensive. I know of a plain boarding house on West Fourteenth Street where you can be accommodated with lodging and two meals—breakfast and supper, or dinner as we call it here—for a dollar a day."

"I shall be glad to go there, for the present, at least. I haven't much money, and must find something to do as soon as possible."

"We will both go there, and if you don't object we will take a room together. That will give us a larger apartment. Mrs. Marcy is an old acquaintance of mine, and will give you a welcome."

Rodney was glad to accept his companion's proposal. They proceeded at once to the boarding house, and fortunately found a good room vacant on the third floor. Mr. Woods went out in the evening to make a call, but Rodney was glad to go to bed at nine o'clock.

The next morning after breakfast Rodney consulted his companion as to what he should do with the casket.

"Do you want to raise money on it?" asked the agent.

"No; I shall not do this unless I am obliged to."

"Have you any idea as to the value of the jewels?"

"No."

"Then I will take you first to a jeweler in Maiden Lane, a friend of mine, who will appraise them. Afterwards I advise you to deposit the casket at a storage warehouse, or get Tiffany to keep it for you."

"I will do as you suggest."

Maiden Lane is a street largely devoted to jewelers, wholesale and retail. Rodney followed Mr. Woods into a store about midway between Broadway and Nassau Street. A pleasant looking man of middle age greeted the agent cordially.

"What can I do for you?" he asked. "Do you wish to buy a diamond ring for the future Mrs. Woods?"

"Not much. I would like to have you appraise some jewelry belonging to my young friend here."

The casket was opened, and the jeweler examined the contents admiringly.

"This is choice jewelry," he said. "Does your friend wish to sell?"

"Not at present," answered Rodney.

"When you do give me a call. I will treat you fairly. You wish me to appraise these articles?"

"Yes, sir, if you will."

"It will take me perhaps fifteen minutes."

The jeweler retired to the back part of the store with the casket.

In about a quarter of an hour he returned.

"Of course I can't give exact figures," he said, "but I value the jewelry at about twelve hundred dollars."

Rodney looked surprised.

"I didn't think it so valuable," he said.

"I don't mean that you could sell it for so much, but if you wish to dispose of it I will venture to give you eleven hundred."

"Thank you. If I decide to sell I will certainly come to you."

"Now," said the agent, "I advise you on the whole to store the casket with Tiffany."

"Shall I have to pay storage in advance?" asked Rodney anxiously.

"I think not. The value of the jewels will be a sufficient guarantee that storage will be paid."

Rodney accompanied Adin Woods to the great jewelry store on the corner of Fifteenth Street and Union Square, and soon transacted his business.

"Now, you won't have any anxiety as to the safety of the casket," said the agent. "Your friend of the train will find it difficult to get hold of the jewels. Now I shall have to leave you, as I have some business to attend to. We will meet at supper."

Rodney decided to call at the office of his late guardian, Benjamin Fielding. It was in the lower part of the city.

On his way down town he purchased a copy of a morning

paper. Almost the first article he glanced at proved to be of especial interest to him. It was headed

SKIPPED TO CANADA

Rumors have been rife for some time affecting the busines standing of Mr. Benjamin Fielding, the well known commission merchant. Yesterday it was discovered that he had left the city, but where he has gone is unknown. It is believed that he is very deeply involved, and seeing no way out of his embarrassment, has skipped to Canada, or perhaps taken passage to Europe. Probably his creditors will appoint a committee to look into his affairs and report what can be done.

LATER—An open letter has been found in Mr. Fielding's desk, addressed to his creditors. It expresses regret for their losses, and promises, if his life is spared, and fortune favors him, to do all in his power to make them good. No one doubts Mr. Fielding's integrity, and regrets are expressed that he did not remain in the city and help unravel the tangle in which his affairs are involved. He is a man of ability, and as he is still in the prime of life, it may be that he will be able to redeem his promises and pay his debts in full, if sufficient time is given him.

"I can get no help or advice from Mr. Fielding," thought Rodney. "I am thrown upon my own resources, and must fight the battle of life as well as I can alone."

He got out in front of the Astor House. As he left the car he soiled his shoes with the mud so characteristic of New York streets.

"Shine your boots?" asked a young Arab, glancing with a business eye at Rodney's spattered shoes.

Rodney accepted his offer, not so much because he thought the blacking would last, as for the opportunity of questioning the free and independent young citizen who was doing, what he hoped to do, that is, making a living for himself.

"Is business good with you?" asked Rodney. "It ought to be with the streets in this condition."

"Yes; me and de Street Commissioner is in league together. He makes business good for me."

"And do you pay him a commission?" asked Rodney smiling.

"I can't tell no official secrets. It might be bad for me."

"You are an original genius."

"Am I? I hope you ain't callin' me names."

"Oh no. I am only paying you a compliment. What is your name?"

"Mike Flynn."

"Where do you live, Mike?"

"At the Lodge."

"I suppose you mean at the Newsboys' 'Lodge?'"

"Yes."

"How much do you have to pay there?"

"Six cents for lodgin', and six cents for supper and breakfast."

"That is, six cents for each."

"Yes; you ain't comin' to live there, are you?" asked Mike.

"I don't know—I may have to."

"You're jokin'."

"What makes you think I am joking?"

"Because you're a swell. Look at them clo'es!"

"I have a good suit of clothes, to be sure, but I haven't much money. You are better off than I am."

"How's that?" asked Mike incredulously.

"You've got work to do, and I am earning nothing."

"If you've got money enough to buy a box and brush, you can go in with me."

"I don't think I should like it, Mike. It would spoil my

clothes, and I am afraid I wouldn't have money enough to buy others."

"I keep my dress suit at home—the one I wear to parties."

"Haven't you got any father or mother, Mike? How does it happen that you are living in New York alone?"

"My farder is dead, and me mudder, she married a man wot ain't no good. He'd bate me till I couldn't stand it. So I just run away."

"Where does your mother live?"

"In Albany."

"Some time when you earn money enough you can ask her to come here and live with you."

"They don't take women at the Lodge."

"No, I suppose not," said Rodney, smiling.

"Besides she's got two little girls by her new husband, and she wouldn't want to leave them."

By this time the shine was completed, and Rodney paid Mike.

"If I ever come to the Lodge, I'll ask for you," he said.

"Where do you live now?"

"I'm just staying at a place on Fourteenth Street, but I can't afford to stay there long, for they charge a dollar a day."

"Geewholliker, that would bust me, and make me a financial wreck as the papers say."

"How did you lose your fortune and get reduced to blacking boots?" asked Rodney jocosely.

"I got scooped out of it in Wall Street," answered Mike. "Jay Gould cleaned me out."

"And I suppose now he has added your fortune to his."

"You've hit it, boss."

"Well, good day, Mike, I'll see you again some day——"

"All right! I'm in my office all de mornin'."

CHAPTER VI.
AN IMPUDENT ADVENTURER.

While Rodney was talking with Mike Flynn he was an object of attention to a man who stood near the corner of Barclay Street, and was ostensibly looking in at the window of the drug store. As Rodney turned away he recognized him at once as his enterprising fellow traveler who had taken possession of the casket of jewels.

He did not care to keep up an acquaintance with him, and started to cross the street. But the other came forward smiling, and with a nod said: "I believe you are the young man I met yesterday in the cars and afterwards at Kentville?"

"Yes, sir."

"I just wanted to tell you that I had got back my jewel box, the one for which I mistook yours."

"Indeed!" said Rodney, who did not believe a word the fellow said.

"Quite an amusing mistake, I made."

"It might have proved serious to me."

"Very true, as I shouldn't have known where to find you to restore your property."

"I don't think that would have troubled you much," thought Rodney. "Where did you find your box?" he asked.

"In the car. That is, the conductor picked it up and left it at the depot for me. Where are you staying here in the city? At the Astor House?"

"No, I have found a boarding house on West Fourteenth Street."

"If it is a good place, I should like to go there. What is the number?"

"I can't recall it, though I could find it," answered Rodney with reserve, for he had no wish to have his railroad acquaintance in the house.

"Is the gentleman who was traveling with you there also?"

"Yes, sir."

"He is a very pleasant gentleman, though he misjudged me. Ha, ha! my friends will be very much amused when I tell them that I was taken for a thief. Why, I venture to say that my box is more valuable than yours."

"Very likely," said Rodney coldly. "Good morning."

"Good morning. I hope we may meet again."

Rodney nodded, but he could not in sincerity echo the wish.

He was now confronted by a serious problem. He had less than ten dollars in his pocketbook, and this would soon be swallowed up by the necessary expenses of life in a large city. What would he do when that was gone?

It was clear that he must go to work as soon as possible. If his guardian had remained in the city, probably through his influence a situation might have been secured. Now nothing was to be looked for in that quarter.

He bought a morning paper and looked over the Want Column. He found two places within a short distance of the Astor House, and called at each. One was in a railroad office.

"My boy," said the manager, a pleasant looking man, "the place was taken hours since. You don't seem to get up very early in the morning."

"I could get up at any hour that was necessary," replied

Rodney, "but I have only just made up my mind to apply for a position."

"You won't meet with any luck today. It is too late. Get up bright and early tomorrow morning, buy a paper, and make early application for any place that strikes you as desirable."

"Thank you, sir. I am sure your advice is good."

"If you had been the first to call here, I should have taken you. I like your appearance better than that of the boy I have selected."

"Thank you, sir."

"This boy may not prove satisfactory. Call in six days, just before his week expires, and if there is likely to be a vacancy I will let you know."

"Thank you, sir. You are very kind."

"I always sympathize with boys. I have two boys of my own."

This conversation quite encouraged Rodney. It seemed to promise success in the future. If he had probably impressed one man, he might be equally fortunate with another.

It was about half past twelve when he passed through Nassau Street.

All at once his arm was grasped, and a cheery voice said, "Where are you going, Rodney?"

"Mr. Woods!" he exclaimed, with pleased recognition.

"Yes, it's your old friend Woods."

"You are not the only railroad friend I have met this morning."

"Who was the other?"

"The gentleman who obligingly took care of my jewel box for a short time."

"You don't mean to say you have met him? Where did you come across him?"

"In front of the Astor House, almost two hours since."

"Did you speak to him?"

"He spoke to me. You will be glad to hear that he has recovered his own casket of jewels."

Adin Woods smiled.

"He must think you are easily imposed upon," he said, "to believe any such story. Anything more?"

"He said his friends would be very much surprised to hear that he had been suspected of theft."

"So he wanted to clear himself with you?"

"Yes; he asked where I was staying."

"I hope you didn't tell him."

"I only said I was at a boarding house on West Fourteenth Street, but didn't mention the number."

"He thinks you have the casket with you, and that he may get possession of it. It is well that you stored it at Tiffany's."

"I think so. Now I have no anxiety about it. Do you think he will find out where we live?"

"Probably, as you gave him a clew. But, Rodney, it is about lunch time, and I confess I have an appetite. Come and lunch with me."

"But I am afraid, Mr. Woods, I shall not be able to return the compliment."

"There is no occasion for it. I feel in good humor this morning. I have sold one lot, and have hopes of disposing of another. The one lot pays me a commission of twenty dollars."

"I wish I could make twenty dollars in a week."

"Sometimes I only sell one lot in a week. It isn't like a regular business. It is precarious. Still, take the year through and I make a pretty good income. Come in here. We can get a good lunch here," and he led the way into a modest restaurant, not far from the site of the old post office, which will be remembered by those whose residence in New York dates back twenty years or more.

"Now we will have a nice lunch," said the agent. "I hope you can do justice to it."

"I generally can," responded Rodney, smiling. "I am seldom troubled with a poor appetite."

"Ditto for me. Now what have you been doing this morning?"

"Looking for a place."

"With what success?"

"Pretty good if I had only been earlier."

Rodney told the story of his application to the manager of the railroad office.

"You will know better next time. I think you'll succeed. I did. When I came to New York at the age of twenty two I had only fifty dollars. That small sum had to last me twelve weeks. You can judge that I didn't live on the fat of the land during that time. I couldn't often eat at Delmonico's. Even Beefsteak John's would have been too expensive for me. However, those old days are over."

The next day and the two following Rodney went about the city making application for positions, but every place seemed full.

On the third day Mr. Woods said, "I shall have to leave you for a week or more, Rodney."

"Where are you going?"

"To Philadelphia. There's a man there who is a capitalist and likes land investments. I am going to visit him, and hope to sell him several lots. He once lived in this city, so he won't object to New York investments."

"I hope you will succeed, Mr. Woods. I think if you are going away I had better give up the room, and find cheaper accommodations. I am getting near the end of my money."

"You are right. It is best to be prudent."

That evening Rodney found a room which he could rent for two dollars a week. He estimated that by economy he could get along for fifty cents a day for his eating, and that would be a decided saving.

He was just leaving the house the next morning, gripsack in hand, when on the steps he met Louis Wheeler, his acquaintance of the train.

"Where are you going?" asked Wheeler.

"I am leaving this house. I have hired a room elsewhere."

Wheeler's countenance fell, and he looked dismayed.

"Why, I have just taken a room here for a week," he said.

"You will find it a good place."

"But—I wouldn't have come here if I hadn't thought I should have company."

"I ought to feel complimented."

Rodney was convinced that Wheeler had come in the hopes of stealing the casket of jewels a second time, and he felt amused at the fellow's discomfiture.

"You haven't got your jewel box with you?"

"No, I can take that another time."

"Then it's still in the house," thought Wheeler with satisfaction. "It won't be my fault if I don't get it in my hands. Well, good morning," he said. "Come around and call on me."

"Thank you!"

CHAPTER VII.
AT THE NEWSBOYS' LODGING HOUSE.

Within a week Rodney had spent all his money, with the exception of about fifty cents. He had made every effort to obtain a place, but without success.

Boys born and bred in New York have within my observation tried for months to secure a position in vain, so it is not surprising that Rodney who was a stranger proved equally unsuccessful.

Though naturally hopeful Rodney became despondent.

"There seems to be no place for me," he said to himself. "When I was at boarding school I had no idea how difficult it is for a boy to earn a living."

He had one resource. He could withdraw the box of jewels from Tiffany's, and sell some article that it contained. But this he had a great objection to doing. One thing was evident, however, he must do something.

His friend, the lot agent, was out of town, and he hardly knew whom to advise with. At last Mike Flynn, the friendly bootblack, whose acquaintance he had made in front of the Astor House, occurred to him.

Mike, humble as he was, was better off than himself. Moreover he was a New York boy, and knew more about "hustling" than Rodney did. So he sought out Mike in his "office."

"Good morning, Mike," said Rodney, as the bootblack was brushing off a customer.

"Oh, it's you, Rodney," said Mike smiling with evident pleasure. "How you're gettin' on?"

"Not at all."

"That's bad. Can I help you? Just say the word, and I'll draw a check for you on the Park Bank."

"Is that where you keep your money?"

"It's one of my banks. You don't think I'd put all my spondulics in one bank, do you?"

"I won't trouble you to draw a check this morning. I only want to ask some advice."

"I've got plenty of that."

"I haven't been able to get anything to do, and I have only fifty cents left. I can't go on like that."

"That's so."

"I've got to give up my room on Fourteenth Street. I can't pay for it any longer. Do you think I could get in at the Lodge?"

"Yes. I'll introduce you to Mr. O'Connor."

"When shall I meet you?"

"At five o'clock. We'll be in time for supper."

"All right."

At five o'clock Mike accompanied Rodney to the large Newsboys' Lodging House on New Chambers Street. Mr. O'Connor, the popular and efficient superintendent, now dead, looked in surprise at Mike's companion. He was a stout man with a kindly face, and Rodney felt that he would prove to be a friend.

"Mr. O'Connor, let me introduce me friend, Mr. Rodney Ropes," said Mike.

"Could you give me a lodging?" asked Rodney in an embarrassed tone.

"Yes; but I am surprised to see a boy of your appearance here."

"I am surprised to be here myself," admitted Rodney.

The superintendent fixed upon him a shrewd, but kindly glance.

"Have you run away from home?" he asked.

"No, sir. It is my home that has run away from me."

"Have you parents?"

"No, sir."

"Do you come from the country?"

"Yes, sir."

"Where have you been living?"

"At a boarding school a few hours from New York."

"Why did you leave it?"

"Because my guardian sent me word that he had lost my fortune, and could no longer pay my bills."

"You have been unfortunate truly. What do you propose to do now?"

"Earn my living if I can. I have been in the city for about two weeks, and have applied at a good many places but in vain."

"Then you were right in coming here. Supper is ready, and although it is not what you are used to, it will satisfy hunger. Mike, you can take Rodney with you."

Within five minutes Rodney was standing at a long table with a bowl of coffee and a segment of bread before him. It wouldn't have been attractive to one brought up to good living, as was the case with him, but he was hungry.

He had eaten nothing since morning except an apple which he had bought at a street stand for a penny, and his stomach urgently craved a fresh supply of food.

Mike stood next to him. The young bootblack, who was used to nothing better, ate his portion with zest, and glanced askance at Rodney to see how he relished his supper. He was surprised to see that his more aristocratic companion seemed to enjoy it quite as much as himself.

"I didn't think you'd like it," he said.

"Anything tastes good when you're hungry, Mike."

"That's so."

"And I haven't eaten anything except an apple, since morning."

"Is dat so? Why didn't you tell me? I'd have stood treat at de Boss Tweed eatin' house."

"I had money, but I didn't dare to spend it. I was afraid of having nothing left."

When Rodney had eaten his supper he felt that he could have eaten more, but the craving was satisfied and he felt relieved.

He looked around him with some curiosity, for he had never been in such a motley gathering before. There were perhaps one hundred and fifty boys recruited from the streets, to about all of whom except himself the term street Arab might be applied.

The majority of them had the shrewd and good humored Celtic face. Many of them were fun loving and even mischievous, but scarcely any were really bad.

Naturally Rodney, with his good clothes, attracted attention. The boys felt that he was not one of them, and they had a suspicion that he felt above them.

"Get on to de dude!" remarked one boy, who was loosely attired in a ragged shirt and tattered trousers.

"He means me, Mike," said Rodney with a smile.

"I say, Patsy Glenn, what do you mean by callin' me friend Rodney a dude?" demanded Mike angrily.

"Coz he's got a dandy suit on."

"What if he has? Wouldn't you wear one like it if you could!"

"You bet!"

"Then just let him alone! He's just got back from de inauguration."

"Where'd you pick him up, Mike?"

"Never mind! He's one of us. How much money have you got in your pocket, Rodney?"

"Thirty two cents."

"He can't put on no frills wid dat money."

"That's so. I take it all back," and Patsy offered a begrimed hand to Rodney, which the latter shook heartily with a pleasant smile.

That turned the tide in favor of Rodney, the boys gathered around him and he told his story in a few words.

"I used to be rich, boys," he said, "but my guardian spent all my money, and now I am as poor as any of you."

"You'd ought to have had me for your guardian, Rodney," observed Mike.

"I wish you had. You wouldn't have lost my money for me."

"True for you! I say so, boys, if we can find Rodney's guardian, what'll we do to him?"

"Give him de grand bounce," suggested Patsy.

"Drop him out of a high winder," said another.

"What's his name?"

"I don't care to tell you, boys. He's written me a letter, saying he will try to pay me back some day. I think he will. He isn't a bad man, but he has been unlucky."

Mike, at the request of Mr. O'Connor, showed Rodney a locker in which he could store such articles of clothing as he had with him. After that he felt more at home, and as if he were staying at a hotel though an humble one.

At eight o'clock some of the boys had already gone to bed, but Mike and Rodney were among those who remained up. Rodney noticed with what kindness yet fairness the superintendent managed his unruly flock. Unruly they might have been with a different man, but he had no trouble in keeping them within bounds.

It was at this time that two strangers were announced, one a New York merchant named Goodnow, the other a tall, slender man with sandy whiskers of the mutton chop pattern.

"Good evening, Mr. Goodnow," said the superintendent, who recognized the merchant as a friend of the society.

"Good evening, Mr. O'Connor. I have brought my friend and correspondent, Mr. Mulgrave, of London, to see some of your young Arabs."

"I shall be glad to give him all the opportunity he desires."

The Englishman looked curiously at the faces of the boys who in turn were examining him with equal interest.

"They are not unlike our boys of a similar grade, but seem sharper and more intelligent," he said. "But surely," pointing to Rodney, "that boy is not one of the—Arabs. Why, he looks like a young gentleman."

"He is a new comer. He only appeared tonight."

"He must have a history. May I speak with him?"

"By all means. Rodney, this gentleman would like to talk with you."

Rodney came forward with the ease of a boy who was accustomed to good society, and said: "I shall be very happy to speak with him."

CHAPTER VIII.
RODNEY FINDS A PLACE.

"Surely," said the Englishman, "you were not brought up in the streets?"

"Oh, no," answered Rodney, "I was more fortunate."

"Then how does it happen that I find you here—among the needy boys of the city?"

"Because I am needy, too."

"But you were not always poor?"

"No; I inherited a moderate fortune from my father. It was only within a short time that I learned from my guardian that it was lost. I left the boarding school where I was being educated, and came to the city to try to make a living."

"But surely your guardian would try to provide for you?"

"He is no longer in the city."

"Who was he?" asked Otis Goodnow.

"Mr. Benjamin Fielding."

"Is it possible? Why, I lost three thousand dollars by him. He has treated you shamefully."

"It was not intentional, I am sure," said Rodney. "He was probably drawn into using my money by the hope of retrieving himself. He wrote me that he hoped at some time to make restitution."

"You speak of him generously, my lad," said Mr. Mulgrave. "Yet he has brought you to absolute poverty."

"Yes, sir, and I won't pretend that it is not a hard trial to me, but if I can get a chance to earn my own living, I will not complain."

"Goodnow, a word with you," said the Englishman, and he drew his friend aside. "Can't you make room for this boy in your establishment?"

Otis Goodnow hesitated. "At present there is no vacancy," he said.

"Make room for him, and draw upon me for his wages for the first six months."

"I will do so, but before the end of that time I am sure he will justify my paying him out of my own pocket."

There was a little further conference, and then the two gentlemen came up to where Rodney was standing with Mr. O'Connor.

"My boy," said Mr. Mulgrave, "my friend here will give you a place at five dollars a week. Will that satisfy you?"

Rodney's face flushed with pleasure.

"It will make me very happy," he said.

"Come round to my warehouse—here is my business card—tomorrow morning," said the merchant. "Ask to see me."

"At what time shall I call, sir?"

"At half past nine o'clock. That is for the first morning. When you get to work you will have to be there at eight."

"There will be no trouble about that, sir."

"Now it is my turn," said the Englishman. "Here are five dollars to keep you till your first week's wages come due. I dare say you will find them useful."

"Thank you very much, sir. I was almost out of money."

After the two gentlemen left the Lodging House Rodney looked at the card and found that his new place of employment was situated on Reade Street not far from Broadway.

"It's you that's in luck, Rodney," said his friend Mike. "Who'd think that a gentleman would come to the Lodging House to give you a place?"

"Yes, I am in luck, Mike, and now I'm going to make you a proposal."

"What is it?"

"Why can't we take a room together? It will be better than living here."

"Sure you wouldn't room with a poor boy like me?"

"Why shouldn't I? You are a good friend, and I should like your company. Besides I mean to help you get an education. I suppose you're not a first class scholar, Mike?"

"About fourth class, I guess, Rodney."

"Then you shall study with me. Then when you know a little more you may get a chance to get out of your present business, and get into a store."

"That will be bully!" said Mike with pleasure.

"Now we'd better go to bed; I must be up bright and early in the morning. We'll engage a room before I go to work."

There was no difficulty about rising early. It is one of the rules of the Lodging House for the boys to rise at six o'clock, and after a frugal breakfast of coffee and rolls they are expected to go out to their business whatever it may be. Mike and Rodney dispensed with the regulation breakfast and went out to a restaurant on Park Row where they fared better.

"Now where shall we go for a room?" asked Rodney.

"There's a feller I know has a good room on Bleecker Street," said Mike.

"How far is that?"

"A little more'n a mile."

"All right! Let us go and see."

Bleecker Street once stood in better repute than at present. It is said that A. T. Stewart once made his home there. Now it is given over to shops and cheap lodging houses.

Finally the boys found a room decently furnished, about ten feet square, of which the rental was two dollars and a half per week. Mike succeeded in beating down the lodging house keeper to two dollars, and at that figure they engaged it.

"When will you come?" asked Mrs. McCarty.

"Right off," said Mike.

"I'll need a little time to put it in order."

"Me and my partner will be at our business till six o'clock," returned Mike.

"You can send in your trunks during the day if you like."

"My trunk is at the Windsor Hotel," said Mike. "I've lent it to a friend for a few days."

Mrs. McCarty looked at Mike with a puzzled expression. She was one of those women who are slow to comprehend a joke, and she could not quite make it seem natural that her new lodger, who was in rather negligé costume, should be a guest at a fashionable hotel.

"I will leave my valise," said Rodney, "and will send for my trunk. It is in the country."

Mike looked at him, not feeling quite certain whether he was in earnest, but Rodney was perfectly serious.

"You're better off than me," said Mike, when they reached the street. "If I had a trunk I wouldn't have anything to put into it."

"I'll see if I can't rig you out, Mike. I've got a good many clothes, bought when I was rich. You and I are about the same size. I'll give you a suit of clothes to wear on Sundays."

"Will you?" exclaimed Mike, his face showing pleasure. "I'd like to see how I look in good clo'es. I never wore any yet. It wouldn't do no good in my business."

"You won't want to wear them when at work. But wouldn't you like to change your business?"

"Yes."

"Have you ever tried?"

"What'd be the use of tryin'? They'd know I was a bootblack in these clo'es."

"When you wear a better suit you can go round and try your luck."

"I'd like to," said Mike wistfully. "I don't want you to tell at the store that you room with a bootblack."

"It isn't that I think of, Mike. I want you to do better. I'm going to make a man of you."

"I hope you are. Sometimes I've thought I'd have to be a bootblack always. When do you think you'll get the clo'es?"

"I shall write to the principal of the boarding school at once, asking him to forward my trunk by express. I want to economize a little this week, and shall have to pay the express charges."

"I'll pay up my part of the rent, Rodney, a quarter a day."

Rodney had advanced the whole sum, as Mike was not in funds.

"If you can't pay a dollar a week I will pay a little more than half."

"There ain't no need. I'll pay my half and be glad to have a nice room."

"I've got three or four pictures at the school, and some books. I'll send for them later on, and we'll fix up the room."

"Will you? We'll have a reg'lar bang up place. I tell you that'll be better than livin' at the Lodge."

"Still that seems a very neat place. It is lucky for poor boys that they can get lodging so cheap."

"But it isn't like havin' a room of your own, Rodney. I say, when we're all fixed I'll ask some of me friends to come in some evenin' and take a look at us. They'll be s'prised."

"Certainly, Mike. I shall be glad to see any of your friends."

It may seem strange that Rodney, carefully as he had been brought up, should have made a companion of Mike, but he recognized in the warm hearted Irish boy, illiterate as he was, sterling qualities, and he felt desirous of helping to educate him. He knew that he could always depend on his devoted friendship, and looked forward with pleasure to their more intimate companionship.

After selecting their room and making arrangements to take possession of it, the boys went down town. Rodney stepped into the reading room at the Astor House and wrote the following letter to Dr. Sampson:

DR. PLINY SAMPSON:

DEAR SIR—Will you be kind enough to send my trunk by express to No. 312 Bleecker Street? I have taken a room there, and that will be my home for the present. I have obtained a position in a wholesale house on Reade Street, and hope I may give satisfaction. Will you remember me with best wishes to all the boys? I don't expect to have so easy or pleasant a time as I had at school, but I hope to get on, and some time—perhaps in the summer—to make you a short visit.

Yours truly,
RODNEY ROPES.

CHAPTER IX.
THE FIRST DAY AT WORK.

A little before half past nine Rodney paused in front of a large five story building on Reade Street, occupied by Otis Goodnow.

He entered and found the first floor occupied by quite a large number of clerks and salesmen, and well filled with goods.

"Well, young fellow, what can I do for you?" asked a dapper looking clerk.

"I would like to see Mr. Goodnow."

"He's reading his letters. He won't see you."

Rodney was provoked.

"Do you decide who is to see him?" he asked.

"You're impudent, young feller."

"Am I? Perhaps you will allow Mr. Goodnow to see me, as long as he told me to call here this morning."

"That's a different thing," returned the other in a different tone. "If you're sure about that, you can go to the office in the back part of the room."

Rodney followed directions and found himself at the entrance of a room which had been partitioned off for the use of the head of the firm.

Mr. Goodnow was seated at a desk with his back to him, and was employed in opening letters. Without turning round he said, "Sit down and I will attend to you in a few minutes."

Rodney seated himself on a chair near the door. In about ten minutes Mr. Goodnow turned around.

"Who is it?" he asked.

"Perhaps you remember telling me to call at half past nine. You saw me at the Newsboys' Lodging House."

"Ah, yes, I remember. I promised my friend Mulgrave that I would give you a place. What can you do? Are you a good writer?"

"Shall I give you a specimen of my handwriting?"

"Yes; sit down at that desk."

It was a desk adjoining his own.

Rodney seated himself and wrote in a firm, clear, neat hand:

"I will endeavor to give satisfaction, if you are kind enough to give me a place in your establishment."

Then he passed over the paper to the merchant.

"Ah, very good!" said Mr. Goodnow approvingly. "You won't be expected to do any writing yet, but I like to take into my store those who are qualified for promotion."

He rang a little bell on his desk.

A boy about two years older than Rodney answered the summons.

"Send Mr. James here," said the merchant.

Mr. James, a sandy complexioned man, partially bald, made his appearance.

"Mr. James," said the merchant, "I have taken this boy into my employ. I don't know if one is needed, but it is at the request of a friend. You can send him on errands, or employ him in any other way."

"Very well, sir. I can find something for him to do today at any rate, as young Johnson hasn't shown up."

"Very well. What's your name, my lad?"

"Rodney Ropes."

"Make a note of his name, Mr. James, and enter it in the books. You may go with Mr. James, and put yourself at his disposal."

Rodney followed the subordinate, who was the head of one of the departments, to the second floor. Here Mr. James had a desk.

"Wait a minute," he said, "and I will give you a memorandum of places to call at."

In five minutes a memorandum containing a list of three places was given to Rodney, with brief instructions as to what he was to do at each. They were places not far away, and fortunately Rodney had a general idea as to where they were.

In his search for positions he had made a study of the lower part of the city which now stood him in good stead.

As he walked towards the door he attracted the attention of the young clerk with whom he had just spoken.

"Well, did you see Mr. Goodnow?" asked the young man, stroking a sickly looking mustache.

"Yes."

"Has he taken you into the firm?"

"Not yet, but he has given me a place."

The clerk whistled.

"So you are one of us?" he said.

"Yes," answered Rodney with a smile.

"Then you ought to know the rules of the house."

"You can tell me later on, but now I am going out on an errand."

In about an hour Rodney returned. He had been detained at two of the places where he called.

"Do you remember what I said?" asked the young clerk as he passed.

"Yes."

"The first rule of the establishment is for a new hand to treat *me* on his first day."

"That's pretty good for you," said Rodney, laughing; "I shall have to wait till my pay is raised."

About the middle of the afternoon, as Rodney was helping to unpack a crate of goods, the older boy whom he had already seen in the office below, walked up to him and said, "Is your name Ropes?"

"Yes."

"You are wanted in Mr. Goodnow's office."

Rodney went down stairs, feeling a little nervous. Had he done wrong, and was he to be reprimanded?

He could think of nothing deserving censure. So far as he knew he had attended faithfully to all the duties required of him.

As he entered the office, he saw that Mr. Goodnow had a visitor, whose face looked familiar to him. He recalled it immediately as the face of the English gentleman who had visited the Lodging House the day previous with his employer.

"So I find you at work?" he said, offering his hand with a smile.

"Yes, sir," answered Rodney gratefully, "thanks to you."

"How do you think you will like it?"

"Very much, sir. It is so much better than going around the streets with nothing to do."

"I hope you will try to give satisfaction to my friend, Mr. Goodnow."

"I shall try to do so, sir."

"You mustn't expect to rise to be head salesman in a year. *Festina lente*, as the Latin poet has it."

"I shall be satisfied with hastening slowly, sir."

"What! you understand Latin?"

"Pretty well, sir."

"Upon my word, I didn't expect to find a boy in the Newsboys' Lodging House with classical attainments. Perhaps you know something of Greek also!" he said doubtfully.

In reply Rodney repeated the first line of the Iliad.

"Astonishing!" exclaimed Mr. Mulgrave, putting up his eyeglass, and surveying Rodney as if he were a curious specimen. "You don't happen to know anything of Sanscrit, do you?"

"No, sir; I confess my ignorance."

"I apprehend you won't require it in my friend Goodnow's establishment."

"If I do, I will learn it," said Rodney, rather enjoying the joke.

"If I write a book about America, I shall certainly put in a paragraph about a learned office boy. I think you are entitled to something for your knowledge of Greek and Latin—say five dollars apiece," and Mr. Mulgrave drew from his pocket two gold pieces and handed them to Rodney.

"Thank you very much, sir," said Rodney. "I shall find this money very useful, as I have taken a room, and am setting up housekeeping."

"Then you have left the Lodging House?"

"Yes, sir; I only spent one night there."

"You are right. It is no doubt a great blessing to the needy street boys, but you belong to a different class."

"It is very fortunate I went there last evening, or I should not have met you and Mr. Goodnow."

"I am glad to have been the means of doing you a service," said the Englishman kindly, shaking hands with Rodney, who bowed and went back to his work.

"I am not sure but you are taking too much notice of that boy, Mulgrave," said the merchant.

"No fear! He is not a common boy. You won't regret employing him."

"I hope not."

Then they talked of other matters, for Mr. Mulgrave was to start on his return to England the following day.

At five o'clock Rodney's day was over, and he went back to Bleecker Street. He found Mike already there, working hard to get his hands clean, soiled as they were by the stains of blacking.

"Did you have a good day, Mike?" asked Rodney.

"Yes; I made a dollar and ten cents. Here's a quarter towards the rent."

"All right! I see you are prompt in money matters."

"I try to be. Do you know, Rodney, I worked better for feelin' that I had a room of my own to go to after I got through. I hope I'll soon be able to get into a different business."

"I hope so, too."

Two days later Rodney's trunk arrived. In the evening he opened it. He took out a dark mixed suit about half worn, and said, "Try that on, Mike."

Mike did so. It fitted as if it were made for him.

"You can have it, Mike," said Rodney.

"You don't mean it?" exclaimed Mike, delighted.

"Yes, I do. I have plenty of others."

Rodney supplemented his gift by a present of underclothing, and on the following Sunday the two boys went to Central Park in the afternoon, Mike so transformed that some of his street friends passed him without recognition, much to Mike's delight.

CHAPTER X.
MIKE PUTS ON A UNIFORM.

A wonderful change came over Mike Flynn. Until he met Rodney he seemed quite destitute of ambition. The ragged and dirty suit which he wore as bootblack were the best he had. His face and hands generally bore the marks of his business, and as long as he made enough to buy three meals a day, two taken at the Lodging House, with something over for lodging, and an occasional visit to a cheap theater, he was satisfied.

He was fifteen, and had never given a thought to what he would do when he was older. But after meeting Rodney, and especially after taking a room with him, he looked at life with different eyes. He began to understand that his business, though honorable because honest, was not a desirable one. He felt, too, that he ought to change it out of regard for Rodney, who was now his close companion.

"If I had ten dollars ahead," he said one day, "I'd give up blackin' boots."

"What else would you do?"

"I'd be a telegraph boy. That's more respectable than blackin' boots, and it 'ould be cleaner."

"That is true. Do you need money to join?"

"I would get paid once in two weeks, and I'd have to live till I got my first salary."

"I guess I can see you through, Mike."

"No; you need all your money, Rodney. I'll wait and see if I can't save it myself."

This, however, would have taken a long time, if Mike had not been favored by circumstances. He was standing near the ladies' entrance to the Astor House one day, when casting his eyes downward he espied a neat pocketbook of Russia leather. He picked it up, and from the feeling judged that it must be well filled.

Now I must admit that it did occur to Mike that he could divert to his own use the contents without detection, as no one had seen him pick it up. But Mike was by instinct an honest boy, and he decided that this would not be right. He thrust it into his pocket, however, as he had no objection to receiving a reward if one was offered.

While he was standing near the entrance, a tall lady, dressed in brown silk and wearing glasses, walked up from the direction of Broadway. She began to peer about like one who was looking for something.

"I guess it's hers," thought Mike.

"Are you looking for anything, ma'am?" he asked.

She turned and glanced at Mike.

"I think I must have dropped my pocketbook," she said. "I had it in my hand when I left the hotel, but I had something on my mind and I think I must have dropped it without noticing. Won't you help me look for it, for I am short sighted?"

"Is this it?" asked Mike, producing the pocketbook.

"Oh yes!" exclaimed the lady joyfully. "Where did you find it?"

"Just here," answered Mike, indicating a place on the sidewalk.

"I suppose there is a good deal of money in it?" said Mike, with pardonable curiosity.

"Then you didn't open it?"

"No, ma'am, I didn't have a chance. I just found it."

"There may be forty or fifty dollars, but it isn't on that account I should have regretted losing it. It contained a receipt for a thousand dollars which I am to use in a law suit. That is very important for it will defeat a dishonest claim for money that I have already paid."

"Then I'm glad I found it."

"You are an honest boy. You seem to be a poor boy also."

"That's true, ma'am. If I was rich I wouldn't black boots for a livin'."

"Dear me, you are one of the young street Arabs I've read about," and the lady looked curiously at Mike through her glasses.

"I expect I am."

"And I suppose you haven't much money."

"My bank account is very low, ma'am."

"I've read a book about a boy named 'Ragged Dick.' I think he was a bootblack, too. Do you know him?"

"He's my cousin, ma'am," answered Mike promptly.

It will be observed that I don't represent Mike as possessed of all the virtues.

"Dear me, how interesting. I bought the book for my little nephew. Now I can tell him I have seen 'Ragged Dick's' cousin. Where is Dick now?"

"He's reformed, ma'am."

"Reformed?"

"Yes, from blackin' boots. He's in better business now."

"If I should give you some of the money in this pocketbook, you wouldn't spend it on drinking and gambling, would you?"

"No, ma'am. I'd reform like my cousin, Ragged Dick."

"You look like a good truthful boy. Here are ten dollars for you."

"Oh, thank you, ma'am! you're a gentleman," said Mike overjoyed. "No, I don't mean that, but I hope you'll soon get a handsome husband."

"My young friend, I don't care to marry, though I appreciate your good wishes. I am an old maid from principle. I am an officer of the Female Suffrage Association."

"Is it a good payin' office, ma'am?" asked Mike, visibly impressed.

"No, but it is a position of responsibility. Please tell me your name that I may make a note of it."

"My name is Michael Flynn."

"I see. You are of Celtic extraction."

"I don't know, ma'am. I never heard that I was. It isn't anything bad, is it?"

"Not at all. I have some Celtic blood in my own veins. If you ever come to Boston you can inquire for Miss Pauline Peabody."

"Thank you, ma'am," said Mike, who thought the lady rather a "queer lot."

"Now I must call upon my lawyer, and leave the receipt which I came so near losing."

"Well, I'm in luck," thought Mike. "I'll go home and dress up, and apply for a position as telegraph boy."

When Rodney came home at supper time he found Mike, dressed in his Sunday suit.

"What's up now, Mike?" he asked. "Have you retired from business?"

"Yes, from the bootblack business. Tomorrow I shall be a telegraph boy."

"That is good. You haven't saved up ten dollars, have you?"

"I saved up two, and a lady gave me ten dollars for findin' her pocketbook."

"That's fine, Mike."

There chanced to be a special demand for telegraph boys at that time, and Mike, who was a sharp lad, on passing the necessary examination, was at once set to work.

He was immensely fond of his blue uniform when he first put it on, and felt that he had risen in the social scale. True, his earnings did not average as much, but he was content with smaller pay, since the duties were more agreeable.

In the evenings under Rodney's instruction he devoted an hour and sometimes two to the task of making up the deficiencies in his early education. These were extensive, but Mike was naturally a smart boy, and after a while began to improve rapidly.

So three months passed. Rodney stood well in with Mr. Goodnow, and was promoted to stock clerk. The discipline which he had received as a student stood him in good stead, and enabled him to make more rapid advancement than some who had been longer in the employ of the firm. In particular he was promoted over the head of Jasper Redwood, a boy two years older than himself, who was the nephew of an old employee who had been for fifteen years in the house.

Jasper's jealousy was aroused, and he conceived a great dislike for Rodney, of which Rodney was only partially aware.

For this dislike there was really no cause. Rodney stood in his way only because Jasper neglected his duties, and failed to inspire confidence. He was a boy who liked to spend money and found his salary insufficient, though he lived with his uncle and paid but two dollars a week for his board.

"Uncle James," he said one day, "when do you think I will get a raise?"

"You might get one now if it were not for the new boy."

"You mean Ropes."

"Yes, he has just been promoted to a place which I hoped to get for you."

"It is mean," grumbled Jasper. "I have been here longer than he."

"True, but he seems to be Mr. Goodnow's pet. It was an unlucky day for you when he got a place in the establishment."

"Did you ask Mr. Goodnow to promote me?"

"Yes, but he said he had decided to give Archer's place to Ropes."

Archer was a young clerk who was obliged, on account of pulmonary weakness, to leave New York and go to Southern California.

"How much does Ropes get now?"

"Seven dollars a week."

"And I only get five, and I am two years older. They ought to have more regard for you, Uncle James, or I, as your nephew, would get promoted."

"I will see what we can do about it."

"I wish Ropes would get into some scrape and get discharged."

It was a new idea, but Jasper dwelt upon it, and out of it grew trouble for Rodney.

CHAPTER XI.
MISSING GOODS.

James Redwood was summoned one morning to the counting room of his employer.

"Mr. Redwood," said the merchant, "I have reason to think that one of my clerks is dishonest."

"Who, sir?"

"That is what I want you to find out."

"What reason have you for suspecting any one?"

"Some ladies' cloaks and some dress patterns are missing."

"Are you sure they were not sold?"

"Yes: the record of sales has been examined, and they are not included."

"That is strange, Mr. Goodnow," said Redwood thoughtfully. "I hope I am not under suspicion."

"Oh, not at all."

"The losses seem to have taken place in my department."

"True, but that doesn't involve you."

"What do you want me to do?"

"Watch those under you. Let nothing in your manner, however, suggest that you are suspicious. I don't want you to put any one on his guard."

"All right, sir. I will be guided by your instructions. Have you any idea how long this has been going on?"

"Only a few weeks."

Mr. Redwood turned to go back to his room, but Mr. Goodnow called him back.

"I needn't suggest to you," he said, "that you keep this to yourself. Don't let any clerk into the secret."

"Very well, sir."

James Redwood, however, did not keep his promise. After supper he called back Jasper as he was about putting on his hat to go out, and said, "Jasper, I wish to speak with you for five minutes."

"Won't it do tomorrow morning? I have an engagement."

"Put it off, then. This is a matter of importance."

"Very well, sir," and Jasper, albeit reluctantly, laid down his hat and sat down.

"Jasper," said his uncle, "there's a thief in our establishment."

Jasper started, and his sallow complexion turned yellower than usual.

"What do you mean, uncle?" he asked nervously.

"What I say. Some articles are missing that have not been sold."

"Such as what?"

"Ladies' cloaks and dress patterns."

"Who told you?" asked Jasper in a low tone.

"Mr. Goodnow."

"What, the boss?"

"Certainly."

"How should he know?"

"I didn't inquire, and if I had he probably wouldn't have told me. The main thing is that he does know."

"He may not be sure."

"He is not a man to speak unless he feels pretty sure."

"I don't see how any one could steal the articles without being detected."

"It seems they are detected."

"Did—did Mr. Goodnow mention any names?"

"No. He wants to watch and find out the thief. I wish you to help me, though I am acting against instructions. Mr. Goodnow asked me to take no one into my confidence. You will see, therefore, that it will be necessary for you to say nothing."

"I won't breathe a word," said Jasper, who seemed to feel more at ease.

"Now that I have told you so much, can you suggest any person who would be likely to commit the theft?"

Jasper remained silent for a moment, then with a smile of malicious satisfaction said, "Yes, I can suggest a person."

"Who is it?"

"The new boy, Rodney Ropes."

James Redwood shook his head.

"I can't believe that it is he. I am not in love with the young fellow, who seems to stand in the way of your advancement, but he seems straight enough, and I don't think it at all likely that he should be the guilty person."

"Yes, Uncle James, he *seems* straight, but you know that still waters run deep."

"Have you seen anything that would indicate guilt on his part?"

"I have noticed this, that, he is very well dressed for a boy of his small salary, and seems always to have money to spend."

"That will count for something. Still he might have some outside means. Have you noticed anything else?"

Jasper hesitated.

"I noticed one evening when he left the store that he had a sizable parcel under his arm."

"And you think it might have contained some article stolen from the stock?"

"That's just what I think now. Nothing of the kind occurred to me at that time, for I didn't know any articles were missing."

"That seems important. When was it that you noticed this?"

"One day last week," answered Jasper hesitatingly.

"Can you remember the day?"

"No."

"Couldn't you fix it some way?"

"No. You see, I didn't attach any particular importance to it at the time, and probably it would not have occurred to me again, but for your mentioning that articles were missing."

"There may be something in what you say," said his uncle thoughtfully. "I will take special notice of young Ropes after this."

"So will I."

"Don't let him observe that he is watched. It would defeat our chances of detecting the thief."

"I'll be careful. Do you want to say anything more, uncle?"

"No. By the way, where were you going this evening?"

"I was going to meet a friend, and perhaps go to the theater. You couldn't lend me a dollar, could you, Uncle James?"

"Yes, I could, but you are not quite able to pay for your own pleasures. It costs all my salary to live, and it's going to be worse next year, for I shall have to pay a higher rent."

"When I have my pay raised, I can get along better."

"If Ropes loses his place, you will probably step into it."

"Then I hope he'll go, and that soon."

When Jasper passed through the front door and stood on the sidewalk, he breathed a sigh of relief.

"So, they are on to us," he said to himself. "But how was it found out? That's what I'd like to know. I have been very careful. I must see Carton at once."

A short walk took him to a billiard room not far from Broadway. A young man of twenty five, with a slight mustache, and a thin, dark face, was selecting a cue.

"Ah, Jasper!" he said. "Come at last. Let us have a game of pool."

"Not just yet. Come outside. I want to speak to you."

Jasper looked serious, and Philip Carton, observing it, made no remonstrance, but taking his hat, followed him out.

"Well, what is it?" he asked.

"Something serious. It is discovered at the store that goods are missing."

"You don't mean it? Are we suspected?"

"No one is suspected—yet."

"But how do you know?"

"My uncle spoke to me about it this evening—just after supper."

"He doesn't think you are in it."

"No."

"How did he find out?"

"Through the boss. Goodnow spoke to him about it today."

"But how should Goodnow know anything about it?"

"That no one can tell but himself. He asked Uncle James to watch the clerks, and see if he could fasten the theft on any of them."

"That is pleasant for us. It is well we are informed so that we can be on our guard. I am afraid our game is up."

"For the present at any rate we must suspend operations. Now, have you some money for me?"

"Well, a little."

"A little? Why there are two cloaks and a silk dress pattern to be accounted for."

"True, but I have to be very careful. I have to submit to a big discount, for the parties I sell to undoubtedly suspect that the articles are stolen."

"Wouldn't it be better to pawn them?"

"It would be more dangerous. Besides you know how liberal pawnbrokers are. I'll tell you what would be better. If I had a sufficient number of articles to warrant it, I could take them on to Boston or Philadelphia, and there would be less risk selling them there."

"That is true. I wish we had thought of that before. Now we shall have to give up the business for a time. How much money have you got for me?"

"Seven dollars."

"Seven dollars!" exclaimed Jasper in disgust. "Why, that is ridiculous. The articles must have been worth at retail a hundred dollars."

"Perhaps so, but I only got fourteen for them. If you think you can do any better you may sell them yourself next time."

"I thought I should assuredly get fifteen dollars out of it," said Jasper, looking deeply disappointed. "I had a use for the money too."

"Very likely. So had I."

"Well, I suppose I must make it do. Listen and I will tell you how I think I can turn this thing to my advantage."

"Go ahead!"

CHAPTER XII.
WHAT WAS FOUND IN RODNEY'S ROOM.

"There is a boy who stands between me and promotion," continued Jasper, speaking in a low tone.

"The boy you mentioned the other day?"

"Yes, Rodney Ropes. Mr. Goodnow got him from I don't know where, and has taken a ridiculous fancy to him. He has been put over my head and his pay raised, though I have been in the store longer than he. My idea is to connect him with the thefts and get him discharged."

"Do you mean that we are to make him a confederate?"

"No," answered Jasper impatiently. "He would be just the fellow to peach and get us all into trouble."

"Then what do you mean?"

"To direct suspicion towards him. We won't do it immediately, but within a week or two. It would do me good to have him turned out of the store."

Jasper proceeded to explain his idea more fully, and his companion pronounced it very clever.

Meanwhile Rodney, not suspecting the conspiracy to deprive him of his place and his good name, worked zealously, encouraged by his promotion, and resolved to make a place for himself which should insure him a permanent connection with the firm.

Ten days passed, and Mr. Redwood again received a summons from the office.

Entering, he found Mr. Goodnow with a letter in his hand.

"Well, Mr. Redwood," he began, "have you got any clew to the party who has stolen our goods?"

"No, sir."

"Has any thing been taken since I spoke with you on the subject?"

"Not that I am aware of."

"Has any one of the clerks attracted your attention by suspicious conduct?"

"No, sir," answered Redwood, puzzled.

"Humph! Cast your eye over this letter."

James Redwood took the letter, which was written in a fine hand, and read as follows:

Mr. Goodnow:

Dear Sir,—I don't know whether you are aware that articles have been taken from your stock, say, ladies' cloaks and silk dress patterns, and disposed of outside. I will not tell you how it has come to my knowledge, for I do not want to get any one's ill will, but I will say, to begin with, that they were taken by one of your employees, and the one, perhaps, that you would least suspect, for I am told that he is a favorite of yours. I may as well say that it is Rodney Ropes. I live near him, and last evening I saw him carry a bundle to his room when he went back from the store. I think if you would send round today when he is out, you would find in his room one or more of the stolen articles. I don't want to get him into trouble, but I don't like to see you robbed, and so I tell you what I know.

A Friend.

Mr. Redwood read this letter attentively, arching his brows, perhaps to indicate his surprise. Then he read it again carefully.

"What do you think of it?" asked the merchant.

"I don't know," answered Redwood slowly.

"Have you ever seen anything suspicious in the conduct of young Ropes?"

"I can't say I have. On the contrary, he seems to be a very diligent and industrious clerk."

"But about his honesty."

"I fancied him the soul of honesty."

"So did I, but of course we are liable to be deceived. It wouldn't be the first case where seeming honesty has been a cover for flagrant dishonesty."

"What do you wish me to do, Mr. Goodnow? Shall I send Ropes down to you?"

"No; it would only give him a chance, if guilty, to cover up his dishonesty."

"I am ready to follow your instructions."

"Do you know where he lodges?"

"Yes, sir."

"Then I will ask you to go around there, and by some means gain admission to his room. If he has any of our goods secreted take possession of them and report to me."

"Very well, sir."

Half an hour later Mrs. McCarty, Rodney's landlady, in response to a ring admitted Mr. James Redwood.

"Does a young man named Ropes lodge here?" he asked.

"Yes, sir."

"I come from the house where he is employed. He has inadvertently left in his room a parcel belonging to us, and I should be glad if you would allow me to go up to his room and take it."

"You see, sir," said Mrs. McCarty in a tone of hesitation, "while you look like a perfect gentleman, I don't know you, and I am not sure whether, in justice to Mr. Ropes, I ought to admit you to his room."

"You are quite right, my good lady; I am sure. It is just what I should wish my own landlady to do. I will therefore ask you to go up to the room with me to see that all is right."

"That seems all right, sir. In that case I don't object. Follow me, if you please."

As they entered Rodney's room Mr. Redwood looked about him inquisitively. One article at once fixed his attention. It was a parcel wrapped in brown paper lying on the bed.

"This is the parcel, I think," he said. "If you will allow me I will open it, to make sure."

Mrs. McCarty looked undecided, but as she said nothing in opposition Mr. Redwood unfastened the strings and unrolled the bundle. His eyes lighted up with satisfaction as he disclosed the contents—a lady's cloak.

Mrs. McCarty looked surprised.

"Why, it's a lady's cloak," she said, "and a very handsome one. What would Mr. Ropes want of such a thing as that?"

"Perhaps he intended to make you a present of it."

"No, he can't afford to make such presents."

"The explanation is simple. It belongs to the store. Perhaps Mr. Ropes left it here inadvertently."

"But he hasn't been here since morning."

"He has a pass key to the front door?"

"Yes, sir."

"Then he may have been here. Would you object to my taking it?"

"Yes, sir, you see I don't know you."

"Your objection is a proper one. Then I will trouble you to take a look at the cloak, so that you would know it again."

"Certainly, sir. I shall remember it!"

"That is all, Mrs. ———?"

"McCarty, sir."

"Mrs. McCarty, I won't take up any more of your time," and Mr. Redwood started to go down stairs.

"Who shall I tell Mr. Ropes called to see him."

"You needn't say. I will mention the matter to him myself. I am employed in the same store."

"All right, sir. Where is the store? I never thought to ask Mr. Ropes."

"Reade Street, near Broadway. You know where Reade Street is?"

"Yes, sir. My husband used to work in Chambers Street. That is the first street south."

"Precisely. Well, I can't stay longer, so I will leave, apologizing for having taken up so much of your time."

"Oh, it's of no consequence, sir."

"He is a perfect gentleman," she said to herself, as Mr. Redwood closed the front door, and went out on the street. "I wonder whether he's a widower."

Being a widow this was quite a natural thought for Mrs. McCarty to indulge in, particularly as Mr. Redwood looked to be a substantial man with a snug income.

Mr. Redwood went back to the store, and went at once to the office.

"Well, Redwood," said Mr. Goodnow, "did you learn anything?"

"Yes, sir."

"Go on."

"I went to the lodging of young Ropes, and was admitted to his room."

"Well?"

"And there, wrapped in a brown paper, I found one of our missing cloaks lying on his bed."

"Is it possible?"

"I am afraid he is not what we supposed him to be, Mr. Goodnow."

"It looks like it. I am surprised and sorry. Do you think he took the other articles that are missing?"

"Of course I can't say, sir, but it is fair to presume that he did."

"I am exceedingly sorry. I don't mind saying, Redwood, that I took an especial interest in that boy. I have already told you the circumstances of my meeting him, and the fancy taken to him by my friend Mulgrave."

"Yes, sir, I have heard you say that."

"I don't think I am easily taken in, and that boy impressed me as thoroughly honest. But of course I don't pretend to be infallible and it appears that I have been mistaken in him."

The merchant looked troubled, for he had come to feel a sincere regard for Rodney. He confessed to himself that he would rather have found any of the other clerks dishonest.

"You may send Ropes to me," he said, "Mr. Redwood, and you will please come with him. We will investigate this matter at once."

"Very well, sir."

CHAPTER XIII.
CHARGED WITH THEFT.

Rodney entered Mr. Goodnow's office without a suspicion of the serious accusation which had been made against him. The first hint that there was anything wrong came to him when he saw the stern look in the merchant's eyes.

"Perhaps," said Mr. Goodnow, as he leaned back in his chair and fixed his gaze on the young clerk, "you may have an idea why I have sent for you."

"No, sir," answered Rodney, looking puzzled.

"You can't think of any reason I may have for wishing to see you?"

"No, sir," and Rodney returned Mr. Goodnow's gaze with honest, unfaltering eyes.

"Possibly you are not aware that within a few weeks some articles have been missed from our stock."

"I have not heard of it. What kind of articles?"

"The boy is more artful than I thought!" soliloquized the merchant.

"All the articles missed," he proceeded, "have been from the room in charge of Mr. Redwood, the room in which you, among others, are employed."

Something in Mr. Goodnow's tone gave Rodney the hint of

the truth. If he had been guilty he would have flushed and showed signs of confusion. As it was, he only wished to learn the truth and he in turn became the questioner.

"Is it supposed," he asked, "that any one in your employ is responsible for these thefts?"

"It is."

"Is any one in particular suspected?"

"Yes."

"Will you tell me who, that is if you think I ought to know?"

"Certainly you ought to know, for it is you who are suspected."

Then Rodney became indignant.

"I can only deny the charge in the most emphatic terms," he said. "If any one has brought such a charge against me, it is a lie."

"You can say that to Mr. Redwood, for it is he who accuses you."

"What does this mean, Mr. Redwood?" demanded Rodney quickly. "What have you seen in me that leads you to accuse me of theft."

"To tell the truth, Ropes, you are about the last clerk in my room whom I would have suspected. But early this morning this letter was received," and he placed in Rodney's hands the letter given in a preceding chapter.

Rodney read it through and handed it back scornfully.

"I should like to see the person who wrote this letter," he said. "It is a base lie from beginning to end."

"I thought it might be when Mr. Goodnow showed it to me," said Redwood in an even tone, "but Mr. Goodnow and I agreed that it would be well to investigate. Therefore I went to your room."

"When, sir?"

"This morning."

"Then it is all right, for I am sure you found nothing."

"On the contrary, Ropes, I found that the statement made in the letter was true. On your bed was a bundle containing one of the cloaks taken from our stock."

Rodney's face was the picture of amazement.

"Is this true?" he said.

"It certainly is. I hope you don't doubt my word."

"Did you bring it back with you?"

"No; your worthy landlady was not quite sure whether I was what I represented, and I left the parcel there. However I opened it in her presence so that she can testify what I found."

"This is very strange," said Rodney, looking at his accuser with puzzled eyes. "I know nothing whatever of the cloak and can't imagine how it got into my room."

"Perhaps it walked there," said Mr. Goodnow satirically.

Rodney colored, for he understood that his employer did not believe him.

"May I go to my room," he asked, "and bring back the bundle with me?"

Observing that Mr. Goodnow hesitated he added, "You can send some one with me to see that I don't spirit away the parcel, and come back with it."

"On these conditions you may go. Redwood, send some one with Ropes."

Rodney followed the chief of his department back to the cloak room, and the latter, after a moment's thought, summoned Jasper.

"Jasper," he said, "Ropes is going to his room to get a parcel which belongs to the store. You may go with him."

There was a flash of satisfaction in Jasper's eyes as he answered with seeming indifference, "All right! I will go. I shall be glad to have a walk."

As the two boys passed out of the store, Jasper asked, "What does it mean, Ropes?"

"I don't know myself. I only know that there is said to be a parcel containing a cloak in my room. This cloak came from the store, and I am suspected of having stolen it."

"Whew! that's a serious matter. Of course it is all a mistake?"

"Yes, it is all a mistake."

"But how could it get to your room unless you carried it there?"

Rodney gave Jasper a sharp look.

"Some one must have taken it there," he said.

"How on earth did Uncle James find out?"

"An anonymous letter was sent to Mr. Goodnow charging me with theft. Did you hear that articles have been missed for some time from the stock?"

"Never heard a word of it," said Jasper with ready falsehood.

"It seems the articles are missing from our room, and some one in the room is suspected of being the thief."

"Good gracious! I hope no one will suspect me," said Jasper in pretended alarm.

"It seems I am suspected. I hope no other innocent person will have a like misfortune."

Presently they reached Rodney's lodgings. Mrs. McCarty was coming up the basement stairs as they entered.

"La, Mr. Ropes!" she said, "what brings you here in the middle of the day?"

"I hear there is a parcel in my room."

"Yes; it contains such a lovely cloak. The gentleman from your store who called a little while ago thought you might have meant it as a present for me."

"I am afraid it will be some time before I can afford to make such presents. Do you know if any one called and left the cloak here?"

"No; I didn't let in no one at the door."

"Was the parcel there when you made the bed?"

"Well, no, it wasn't. That is curious."

"It shows that the parcel has been left here since. Now I certainly couldn't have left it, for I have been at work all the morning. Come up stairs, Jasper."

The two boys went up the stairs, and, entering Rodney's room, found the parcel, still on the bed.

Rodney opened it, and identified the cloak as exactly like those which they carried in stock.

He examined the paper in which it was inclosed, but it seemed to differ from the wrapping paper used at the store. He called Jasper's attention to this.

"I have nothing to say," remarked Jasper, shrugging his shoulders. "I don't understand the matter at all. I suppose you are expected to carry the cloak back to the store."

"Yes, that is the only thing to do."

"I say, Ropes, it looks pretty bad for you."

Jasper said this, but Rodney observed that his words were not accompanied by any expressions of sympathy, or any words that indicated his disbelief of Rodney's guilt.

"Do you think I took this cloak from the store?" he demanded, facing round upon Jasper.

"Really, I don't know. It looks bad, finding it in your room."

"I needn't ask any further. I can see what you think."

"You wouldn't have me tell a lie, would you, Ropes? Of course such things have been done before, and your salary is small."

"You insult me by your words," said Rodney, flaming up.

"Then I had better not speak, but you asked me, you know."

"Yes, I did. Things may look against me, but I am absolutely innocent."

"If you can make Mr. Goodnow think so," said Jasper with provoking coolness, "it will be all right. Perhaps he will forgive you."

"I don't want his forgiveness. I want him to think me honest."

"Well, I hope you are, I am sure, but it won't do any good our discussing it, and it doesn't make any difference what I think any way."

By this time they had reached the store.

CHAPTER XIV.
RODNEY IS DISCHARGED.

Rodney reported his return to Mr. Redwood, and in his company went down stairs to the office, with the package under his arm.

"Well?" said Mr. Goodnow inquiringly.

"This is the package, sir."

"And it was found in your room?"

"Yes, sir, I found it on my bed."

"Can't you account for its being there?" asked the merchant searchingly.

"No, sir."

"You must admit that its presence in your room looks bad for you."

"I admit it, sir; but I had nothing to do with its being there."

"Have you any theory to account for it?"

"Only this, that some one must have carried it to my room and placed it where it was found."

"Did you question your landlady as to whether she had admitted any one during the morning?"

"Yes, sir. She had not."

"This is very unfavorable to you."

"In what way, sir?"

"It makes it probable that you carried in the parcel yourself."

"That I deny," said Rodney boldly.

"I expected you to deny it," said the merchant coldly. "If this cloak were the only one that had been taken I would drop the matter. But this is by no means the case. Mr. Redwood, can you give any idea of the extent to which we have been robbed?"

"So far as I can estimate we have lost a dozen cloaks and about half a dozen dress patterns."

"This is a serious loss, Ropes," said Mr. Goodnow. "I should think it would foot up several hundred dollars. If you can throw any light upon the thefts, or give me information by which I can get back the goods even at considerable expense, I will be as considerate with you as I can."

"Mr. Goodnow," returned Rodney hotly, "I know no more about the matter than you do. I hope you will investigate, and if you can prove that I took any of the missing articles I want no consideration. I shall expect you to have me arrested, and, if convicted, punished."

"These are brave words, Ropes," said Mr. Goodnow coldly, "but they are only words. The parcel found in your room affords strong ground for suspicion that you are responsible for at least a part of the thefts. Under the circumstances there is only one thing for me to do, and that is to discharge you."

"Very well, sir."

"You may go to the cashier and he will pay you to the end of the week, but your connection with the store will end at once."

"I don't care to be paid to the end of the week, sir. If you will give me an order for payment up to tonight, that will be sufficient."

"It shall be as you say."

Mr. Goodnow wrote a few words on a slip of paper and handed it to Rodney.

"I will leave my address, sir, and if I change it I will notify you. If you should hear anything as to the real robber I will ask you as a favor to communicate with me."

"Mr. Redwood, you have heard the request of Ropes, I will look to you to comply with it."

"Very well, sir."

The merchant turned back to his letters, and Rodney left the office, with what feelings of sorrow and humiliation may be imagined.

"I am sorry for this occurrence, Ropes," said Mr. Redwood, with a touch of sympathy in his voice.

"Do you believe me guilty, Mr. Redwood?"

"I cannot do otherwise. I hope you are innocent, and, if so, that the really guilty party will be discovered sooner or later."

"Thank you, sir."

When they entered the room in which Rodney had been employed Jasper came up, his face alive with curiosity.

"Well," he said, "how did you come out?"

"I am discharged," said Rodney bitterly.

"Well, you couldn't complain of that. Things looked pretty dark for you."

"If I had committed the theft, I would not complain. Indeed, I would submit to punishment without a murmur. But it is hard to suffer while innocent."

"Uncle James," said Jasper, "if Ropes is going will you ask Mr. Goodnow to put me in his place?"

Even Mr. Redwood was disgusted by this untimely request.

"It would be more becoming," he said sharply, "if you would wait till Ropes was fairly out of the store before applying for his position."

"I want to be in time. I don't want any one to get ahead of me."

James Redwood did not deign a reply.

"I am sorry you leave us under such circumstances, Ropes,"

he said. "The time may come when you will be able to establish your innocence, and in that case Mr. Goodnow will probably take you back again."

Rodney did not answer, but with his order went to the cashier's desk and received the four dollars due him. Then, with a heavy heart, he left the store where it had been such a satisfaction to him to work.

On Broadway he met his room mate, Mike Flynn, in the uniform of a telegraph boy.

"Where are you goin', Rodney?" asked Mike. "You ain't let off so early, are you?"

"I am let off for good and all, Mike."

"What's that?"

"I am discharged."

"What for?" asked Mike in amazement.

"I will tell you when you get home tonight."

Rodney went back to his room, and lay down sad and despondent. Some hours later Mike came in, and was told the story. The warm hearted telegraph boy was very angry.

"That boss of yours must be a stupid donkey," he said.

"I don't know. The parcel was found in my room."

"Anybody'd know to look at you that you wouldn't steal."

"Some thieves look very innocent. The only way to clear me is to find out who left the bundle at the house."

"Doesn't Mrs. McCarty know anything about it?"

"No; I asked her."

"Some one might have got into the house without her knowing anything about it. The lock is a very common one. There are plenty of keys that will open it."

"If we could find some one that saw a person with a bundle go up the steps, that would give us a clew."

"That's so. We'll ask."

But for several days no one could be found who had seen any such person.

Meanwhile Rodney was at a loss what to do. He was cut off from applying for another place, for no one would engage him if he were refused a recommendation from his late employer. Yet he must obtain some employment, for he could not live on nothing.

"Do you think, Mike," he asked doubtfully, "that I could make anything selling papers?"

"Such business isn't for you," answered the telegraph boy.

"But it is one of the few things open to me. I can become a newsboy without recommendations. Even your business would be closed to me if it were known that I was suspected of theft."

"That's so," said Mike, scratching his head in perplexity.

"Then would you recommend my becoming a newsboy?"

"I don't know. You couldn't make more'n fifty or sixty cents a day."

"That will be better than nothing."

"And I can pay the rent, or most of it, as I'll be doin' better than you."

"We will wait and see how much I make."

So Rodney swallowed his pride, and procuring a supply of afternoon papers set about selling them. He knew that it was an honest business, and there was no disgrace in following it.

But one day he was subjected to keen mortification. Jasper Redwood and a friend—it was Philip Carton, his confederate —were walking along Broadway, and their glances fell on Rodney.

"I say, Jasper," said the elder of the two, "isn't that the boy who was in the same store with you?"

Jasper looked, and his eyes lighted up with malicious satisfaction.

"Oho!" he said. "Well, this is rich!"

"Give me a paper, boy," he said, pretending not to recognize Rodney at first. "Why, it's Ropes."

1. The single illustration from the *Argosy* serialization of *Cast upon the Breakers*. The original caption read "Rodney examined the locket and his heart was saddened." This is the only known picture of the last Alger hero.

2. Among Alger's heroes were country boys and city waifs. All were honest, enterprising, respectful and handy with their fists. Dozens of bullies rued the day they took a swing at one of these robust lads. Illustration from *Jack's Ward*.

3. In Chicago, Luke Walton took time out from selling newspapers **at** corner of Clark and Randolph Streets to rescue an elderly lady from swiftly approaching horsecar. From *Luke Walton*.

4. Episodes of bravery highlighted every Alger story. In *Brave and Bold*, hero Robert Rushton risks his life to flag down a train "speeding towards him at the rate of twenty-five miles an hour!"

5. On the sidewalks of New York, Paul the Peddler sold prize packages before becoming a necktie merchant on his way to the top. From *Paul the Peddler*.

6. Not all Alger heroes were good, at least at the start of their careers. Here a hero from *Mark the Match Boy* takes a puff of tobacco.

RAGGED DICK SERIES

BY

HORATIO ALGER JR,

7. Ragged Dick is the hero that first gained wide fame for Alger. Here is the title page from the *Ragged Dick* series.

Strive and Succeed! The world's temptations flee
Be Brave and Bold! and Strong and Steady be!
Shift for yourself, and prosper then you must!
Win Fame and Fortune while you Try and Trust!
                                   Horatio Alger Jr.

Feb. 22? 1890.

If I would have my name endure
I'll write it on the hearts of men
In characters of living light
Form kindly deeds and actions
        thought;
And these, beyond the reach of Time,
Shall live, immortal as my thought.
                    Horatio Alger Jr.

Feb 25. 1892.

8. Two specimens of Horatio Alger's handwriting. At top is a poem he composed of the titles of several of his books. At bottom, the final stanza of "Carving a Name," the author's favorite poem. It was for years reprinted in "reciters," "popular programs" and school texts.

"Yes," answered Rodney, his cheek flushing. "You see what I am reduced to. What paper will you buy?"

"The *Mail and Express*."

"Here it is."

"Can't you get another place?" asked Jasper curiously.

"I might if I could get a recommendation, but probably Mr. Goodnow wouldn't give me one."

"No, I guess not."

"So I must take what I can get."

"Do you make much selling papers?"

"Very little."

"You can't make as much as you did in the store?"

"Not much more than half as much."

"Do you live in the same place?"

"Yes, for the present."

"Oh, by the way, Ropes, I've got your old place," said Jasper in exultation.

"I thought you would get it," answered Rodney, not without a pang.

"Come into the store some day, Ropes. It will seem like old times."

"I shall not enter the store till I am able to clear myself of the charge made against me."

"Then probably you will stay away a long time."

"I am afraid so."

"Well, ta, ta! Come along, Philip."

As Rodney followed with his eye the figure of his complacent successor he felt that his fate was indeed a hard one.

CHAPTER XV.
A RICH FIND.

As Jasper and his companion moved away, Carton said, "I'm sorry for that poor duffer, Jasper."

"Why should you be sorry?" asked Jasper, frowning.

"Because he has lost a good place and good prospects, and all for no fault of his own."

"You are getting sentimental, Philip," sneered Jasper.

"No, but I am showing a little humanity. He has lost all this through you——"

"Through us, you mean."

"Well, through us. We have made him the scapegoat for our sins."

"Oh well, he is making a living."

"A pretty poor one. I don't think you would like to be reduced to selling papers."

"His case and mine are different."

"I begin to think also that we have made a mistake in getting him discharged so soon."

"We can't take anything more."

"Why not?"

"Because there will be no one to lay the blame upon. He is out of the store."

"That is true. I didn't think of that. But I invited him to come around and call. If he should, and something else should be missing it would be laid to him."

"I don't believe he will call. I am terribly hard up, and our source of income has failed us. Haven't you got a dollar or two to spare?"

"No," answered Jasper coldly. "I only get seven dollars a week."

"But you have nearly all that. You only have to hand in two dollars a week to your uncle."

"Look here, Philip Carton, I hope you don't expect to live off me. I have all I can do to take care of myself."

Carton looked at Jasper in anger and mortification.

"I begin to understand how good a friend you are," he said.

"I am not fool enough to pinch myself to keep you," said Jasper bluntly. "You are a man of twenty five and I am only a boy. You ought to be able to take care of yourself."

"Just give me a dollar, or lend it, Jasper, and I will risk it at play. I may rise from the table with a hundred. If I do I will pay you handsomely for the loan."

"I couldn't do it, Mr. Carton. I have only two dollars in my pocket, and I have none to spare."

"Humph! what is that?"

Philip Carton's eyes were fixed upon the sidewalk. There was a flimsy piece of paper fluttering about impelled by the wind. He stooped and picked it up.

"It is a five dollar bill," he exclaimed in exultation. "My luck has come back."

Jasper changed his tone at once. Now Philip was the better off of the two.

"That is luck!" he said. "Shall we go into Delmonico's, and have an ice?"

"If it is at your expense, yes."

"That wouldn't be fair. You have more money than I."

"Yes, and I mean to keep it myself. You have set me the example."

"Come, Philip, you are not angry at my refusing you a loan?"

"No; I think you were sensible. I shall follow your example. I will bid you good night. I seem to be in luck, and will try my fortune at the gaming table."

"I will go with you."

"No; I would prefer to go alone."

"That fellow is unreasonable," muttered Jasper, as he strode off, discontented. "Did he expect I would divide my salary with him?"

Philip Carton, after he parted company with Jasper, walked back to where Rodney was still selling papers.

"Give me a paper," he said.

"Which will you have?"

"I am not particular. Give me the first that comes handy. Ah, the *Evening Sun* will do."

He took the paper and put a quarter into Rodney's hand.

As he was walking away Rodney called out, "Stop, here's your change."

"Never mind," said Philip with a wave of the hand.

"Thank you," said Rodney gratefully, for twenty five cents was no trifle to him at this time.

"That ought to bring me luck," soliloquized Philip Carton as he walked on. "It isn't often I do a good deed. It was all the money I had besides the five dollar bill, and I am sure the newsboy will make better use of it than I would."

"That was the young man that was walking with Jasper," reflected Rodney. "Well, he is certainly a better fellow than he. Thanks to this quarter, I shall have made eighty cents today, and still have half a dozen papers. That is encouraging."

Several days passed that could not be considered lucky. Rodney's average profits were only about fifty cents a day, and that was barely sufficient to buy his meals. It left him nothing to put towards paying room rent.

He began to consider whether he would not be compelled to pawn some article from his wardrobe, for he was well supplied with clothing, when he had a stroke of luck.

On Fifteenth Street, by the side of Tiffany's great jewelry store, he picked up a square box neatly done up in thin paper. Opening it, he was dazzled by the gleam of diamonds.

The contents were a diamond necklace and pin, which, even to Rodney's inexperienced eyes, seemed to be of great value.

"Some one must have dropped them in coming from the jewelry store," he reflected. "Who can it be?"

He had not far to seek. There was a card inside on which was engraved:

MRS. ELIZA HARVEY,

with an address on Fifth Avenue.

Passing through to Fifth Avenue Rodney began to scan the numbers on the nearest houses. He judged that Mrs. Harvey must live considerably farther up the Avenue, in the direction of Central Park.

"I will go there at once," Rodney decided. "No doubt Mrs. Harvey is very much distressed by her loss. I shall carry her good news."

The house he found to be between Fortieth and Fiftieth Streets. Ascending the steps he rang the bell. The door was opened by a man servant.

"Does Mrs. Harvey live here?" asked Rodney.

"What do you want with her, young man?" demanded the servant in a tone of importance.

"That I will tell her."

"What's your name?"

"I can give you my name, but she won't recognize it."

"Then you don't know her."

"No."

"If it's money you want, she don't give to beggars."

"You are impudent," said Rodney hotly. "If you don't give my message you will get into trouble."

The servant opened his eyes. He seemed somewhat impressed by Rodney's confident tone.

"Mrs. Harvey doesn't live here," he said.

"Is she in the house?"

"Well, yes, she's visiting here."

"Then why do you waste your time?" said Rodney impatiently. He forgot for the time that he was no longer being educated at an expensive boarding school, and spoke in the tone he would have used before his circumstances had changed.

"I'll go and ask if she'll see you," said the flunky unwillingly.

Five minutes later a pleasant looking woman of middle age descended the staircase.

"Are you the boy that wished to see me?" she asked.

"Yes, if you are Mrs. Harvey."

"I am. But come in! Thomas, why didn't you invite this young gentleman into the parlor?"

Thomas opened his eyes wide. So the boy whom he had treated so cavalierly was a young gentleman.

He privately put down Mrs. Harvey in his own mind as eccentric.

"Excuse me, ma'am," he said. "I didn't know as he was parlor company."

"Well, he is," said Mrs. Harvey with a cordial smile that won Rodney's heart.

"Follow me!" said the lady.

Rodney followed her into a handsome apartment and at a signal seated himself on a sofa.

"Now," she said, "I am ready to listen to your message."

"Have you lost anything?" asked Rodney abruptly.

"Oh, have you found it?" exclaimed Mrs. Harvey, clasping her hands.

"That depends on what you have lost," answered Rodney, who felt that it was necessary to be cautious.

"Certainly, you are quite right. I have lost a box containing jewelry bought this morning at Tiffany's."

"What were the articles?"

"A diamond necklace and pin. They are intended as a present for my daughter who is to be married. Tell me quick, have you found them?"

"Is this the box?" asked Rodney.

"Oh yes, yes! How delightful to recover it. I thought I should never see it again. Where did you find it?"

"On Fifteenth Street beside Tiffany's store."

"And you brought it directly to me?"

"Yes, madam."

"Have you any idea of the value of the articles?"

"Perhaps they may be worth five hundred dollars."

"They are worth over a thousand. Are you poor?"

"Yes, madam. I am trying to make a living by selling papers, but find it hard work."

"But you don't look like a newsboy."

"Till a short time since I thought myself moderately rich."

"That is strange. Tell me your story."

CHAPTER XVI.
A SURPRISING TURN OF FORTUNE.

Rodney told his story frankly. Mrs. Harvey was very sympathetic by nature, and she listened with the deepest interest, and latterly with indignation when Rodney spoke of his dismissal from Mr. Goodnow's store.

"You have been treated shamefully," she said warmly.

"I think Mr. Goodnow really believes me guilty," rejoined Rodney.

"A dishonest boy would hardly have returned a valuable box of jewelry."

"Still Mr. Goodnow didn't know that I would do it."

"I see you are disposed to apologize for your late employer."

"I do not forget that he treated me kindly till this last occurrence."

"Your consideration does you credit. So you have really been reduced to earn your living as a newsboy?"

"Yes, madam."

"I must think what I can do for you. I might give you money, but when that was gone you would be no better off."

"I would much rather have help in getting a place."

Mrs. Harvey leaned her head on her hand and looked thoughtful.

"You are right," she said. "Let me think."

Rodney waited, hoping that the lady would be able to think of something to his advantage.

Finally she spoke.

"I think you said you understood Latin and Greek?"

"I have studied both languages and French also. I should have been ready to enter college next summer."

"Then perhaps I shall be able to do something for you. I live in Philadelphia, but I have a brother living in West Fifty Eighth Street. He has one little boy, Arthur, now nine years of age. Arthur is quite precocious, but his health is delicate, and my brother has thought of getting a private instructor for him. Do you like young children?"

"Very much. I always wished that I had a little brother."

"Then I think you would suit my brother better as a tutor for Arthur than a young man. Being a boy yourself, you would be not only tutor but companion."

"I should like such a position very much."

"Then wait here a moment, and I will write you a letter of introduction."

She went up stairs, but soon returned.

She put a small perfumed billet into Rodney's hands. It was directed to John Sargent, with an address on West Fifty Eighth Street.

"Call this evening," she said, "about half past seven o'clock. My brother will be through dinner, and will not have gone out at that hour."

"Thank you," said Rodney gratefully.

"Here is another envelope which you can open at your leisure. I cannot part from you without thanking you once more for returning my jewelry."

"You have thanked me in a very practical way, Mrs. Harvey."

"I hope my letter may lead to pleasant results for you. If

you ever come to Philadelphia call upon me at No. 1492 Wal-
nut Street."

"Thank you."

As Rodney left the house he felt that his ill fortune had
turned, and that a new prospect was opened up before him. He
stepped into the Windsor Hotel, and opened the envelope last
given him. It contained five five dollar bills.

To one of them was pinned a scrap of paper containing
these words: "I hope this money will be useful to you. It is less
than the reward I should have offered for the recovery of the
jewels."

Under the circumstances Rodney felt that he need not scruple
to use the money. He knew that he had rendered Mrs. Harvey
a great service, and that she could well afford to pay him the
sum which the envelopes contained.

He began to be sensible that he was hungry, not having
eaten for some time. He went into a restaurant on Sixth Avenue, and ordered a sirloin steak. It was some time since he had
indulged in anything beyond a common steak, and he greatly
enjoyed the more luxurious meal. He didn't go back to selling
papers, for he felt that it would hardly be consistent with the
position of a classical teacher—the post for which he was about
to apply.

Half past seven found him at the door of Mr. John Sargent.
The house was of brown stone, high stoop, and four stories
in height. It was such a house as only a rich man could occupy.

He was ushered into the parlor and presently Mr. Sargent
came in from the dining room.

"Are you Mr. Ropes?" he asked, looking at Rodney's card.

It is not usual for newsboys to carry cards, but Rodney had
some left over from his more prosperous days.

"Yes, sir. I bring you a note of introduction from Mrs. Harvey."

"Ah yes, my sister. Let me see it."

The note was of some length. That is, it covered three pages of note paper. Mr. Sargent read it attentively.

"My sister recommends you as tutor for my little son, Arthur," he said, as he folded up the letter.

"Yes, sir; she suggested that I might perhaps suit you in that capacity."

"She also says that you found and restored to her a valuable box of jewelry which she was careless enough to drop near Tiffany's."

"Yes, sir."

"I have a good deal of confidence in my sister's good judgment. She evidently regards you very favorably."

"I am glad of that, sir."

"Will you tell me something of your qualifications? Arthur is about to commence Latin. He is not old enough for Greek."

"I could teach either, sir."

"And of course you are well up in English branches?"

"I think I am."

"My sister hints that you are poor, and obliged to earn your own living. How, then, have you been able to secure so good an education?"

"I have only been poor for a short time. My father left me fifty thousand dollars, but it was lost by my guardian."

"Who was your guardian?"

"Mr. Benjamin Fielding."

"I knew him well. I don't think he was an unprincipled man, but he was certainly imprudent, and was led into acts that were reprehensible. Did he lose all your money for you?"

"Yes, sir."

"What did you do?"

"Left the boarding school where I was being educated, and came to this city."

"Did you obtain any employment?"

"Yes, sir; I have been employed for a short time by Otis Goodnow, a merchant of Reade Street."

"And why did you leave?"

"Because Mr. Goodnow missed some articles from his stock, and I was charged with taking them."

Rodney was fearful of the effect of his frank confession upon Mr. Sargent, but the latter soon reassured him.

"Your honesty in restoring my sister's jewelry is sufficient proof that the charge was unfounded. I shall not let it influence me."

"Thank you, sir."

"Now as to the position of teacher, though very young, I don't see why you should not fill it satisfactorily. I will call Arthur."

He went to the door and called "Arthur."

A delicate looking boy with a sweet, intelligent face, came running into the room.

"Do you want me, papa?"

"Yes, Arthur. I have a new friend for you. Will you shake hands with him?"

Arthur, who was not a shy boy, went up at once to Rodney and offered his hand.

"I am glad to see you," he said.

Rodney smiled. He was quite taken with the young boy.

"What's your name?" the latter asked.

"Rodney Ropes."

"Are you going to stay and make us a visit?"

Mr. Sargent answered this question.

"Would you like to have Rodney stay?" he asked.

"Oh yes."

"How would you like to have him give you lessons in Latin and other studies?"

"I should like it. I am sure he wouldn't be cross. Are you a teacher, Rodney?"

"I will be your teacher if you are willing to have me."

"Yes, I should like it. And will you go to walk with me in Central Park?"

"Yes."

"Then, papa, you may as well engage him. I was afraid you would get a tiresome old man for my teacher."

"That settles it, Rodney," said Mr. Sargent, smiling. "Now, Arthur, run out, and I will speak further with Rodney about you."

"All right, papa."

"As Arthur seems to like you, I will give you a trial. As he suggested, I should like to have you become his companion as well as teacher. You will come here at nine o'clock in the morning, and stay till four, taking lunch with your pupil. About the compensation, will you tell me what will be satisfactory to you?"

"I prefer to leave that to you, sir."

"Then we will say fifteen dollars a week—today is Thursday. Will you present yourself here next Monday morning?"

"Yes, sir."

"If you would like an advance of salary, you need only say so."

"Thank you, sir, but I am fairly provided with money for the present."

"Then nothing more need be said. As I am to meet a gentleman at the Union League Club tonight, I will bid you good evening, and expect to see you on Monday."

Rodney rose and Mr. Sargent accompanied him to the door, shaking hands with him courteously by way of farewell.

Rodney emerged into the street in a state of joyous excitement. Twenty five dollars in his pocket, and fifteen dollars a week! He could hardly credit his good fortune.

CHAPTER XVII.
JASPER'S PERPLEXITY.

Mike Flynn was overjoyed to hear of Rodney's good fortune.

"Fifteen dollars a week!" he repeated. "Why you will be rich."

"Not exactly that, Mike, but it will make me comfortable. By the way, as I have so much more than you, it will only be fair for me to pay the whole rent."

"No, Rodney, you mustn't do that."

"I shall insist upon it, Mike. You would do the same in my place."

"Yes I would."

"So you can't object to my doing it."

"You are very kind to me, Rodney," said Mike, who had the warm heart of his race. "It isn't every boy brought up like you who would be willing to room with a bootblack."

"But you are not a bootblack now. You are a telegraph boy."

"There are plenty that mind me when I blacked boots down in front of the Astor House."

"You are just as good a boy for all that. How much did you make last week?"

"Four dollars salary, and a dollar and a half in extra tips."

"Hereafter you must save your rent money for clothes. We must have you looking respectable."

"Won't you adopt me, Rodney?" asked Mike with a laughing face.

"That's a good idea. Perhaps I will. In that case you must obey all my orders. In the first place, what are you most in want in the way of clothing?"

"I haven't got but two shirts."

"That is hardly enough for a gentleman of your social position. Anything else."

"I'm short on collars and socks."

"Then we'll go out shopping. I'll buy you a supply of each."

"But you haven't begun to work yet."

"No, but Mrs. Harvey made me a present of twenty five dollars. We'll go to some of the big stores on Sixth Avenue where we can get furnishing goods cheap."

Rodney carried out his purpose, and at the cost of four dollars supplied his room mate with all he needed for the present.

"See what it is to be rich, Mike," he said. "It seems odd for me to be buying clothes for my adopted son."

"You're in luck, Rodney, and so am I. I hope some time I can do you a favor."

"Perhaps you can, Mike. If I should get sick, you might take my place as tutor."

"You must know an awful lot, Rodney," said Mike, regarding his companion with new respect.

"Thank you for the compliment, Mike. I hope Mr. Sargent will have the same opinion."

The next day it is needless to say that Rodney did not resume the business of newsboy. He was very glad to give it up. He dressed with unusual care and took a walk down town.

As he passed Reade Street by chance Jasper was coming around the corner. His face lighted up first with pleasure at seeing Rodney, for it gratified his mean nature to triumph over the boy whom he had ousted from his position, and next with surprise at his unusually neat and well dressed appearance. Rodney looked far from needing help. He might readily have been taken for a boy of aristocratic lineage.

"Hallo!" said Jasper, surveying Rodney curiously.

"How are you this morning, Jasper?" returned Rodney quietly.

"Why ain't you selling papers?"

"I don't like the business."

"But you've got to make a living."

"Quite true."

"Are you going to black boots?"

"Why should I? Is it a desirable business?"

"How should I know?" asked Jasper, coloring.

"I didn't know but you might have had some experience at it. I haven't."

"Do you mean to insult me?" demanded Jasper hotly.

"I never insult anybody. I will only say that you are as likely to take up the business as I."

"I've got a place."

"How do you know but I have?"

"Because you were selling papers yesterday and are walking the streets today."

"That is true. But I have a place engaged for all that. I shall go to work on Monday."

Jasper pricked up his ears.

"Where is it?" he asked.

"I don't care to tell at present."

"Is it true? Have you got a place?"

"Yes."

"I don't see how you could. Mr. Goodnow wouldn't give you a recommendation."

"There is no reason why he should not."

"What, after your taking cloaks and dress patterns from the store?"

"I did nothing of the kind. Sooner or later Mr. Goodnow will find out his mistake. Probably the real thief is still in his employ."

Jasper turned pale and regarded Rodney searchingly, but there was nothing in his manner or expression to indicate that his remark had been personal. He thought it best to turn the conversation.

"How much pay do you get—four dollars?"

"More than that."

"You don't get as much as you did at our store?"

"Yes; I get more."

Now it was Jasper's turn to show surprise. He did not know whether to believe Rodney or not, but there was something in his face which commanded belief.

"How much do you get?" he asked.

"You would not believe me if I told you."

"Try me," returned Jasper, whose curiosity was aroused.

"I am to get fifteen dollars a week."

Jasper would not have looked more surprised if Rodney had informed him that he was to become a Cabinet minister.

"You're joking!" he ejaculated.

"Not at all."

"How could you have the face to ask such a price. Did you pass yourself off as an experienced salesman?"

"No."

"I don't understand it at all, that is, if you are telling the truth."

"I have told you the truth, Jasper. I have no object in deceiving you. The salary was fixed by my employer."

"Who did you say it was?"

"I didn't say."

Jasper's cunning scheme was defeated. He felt disturbed to hear of Rodney's good fortune, but he had a shot in reserve.

"I don't think you will keep your place long," he said in a malicious tone.

"Why not?"

"Your employer will hear under what circumstances you left our store, and then of course he will discharge you."

"You will be sorry for that, won't you?" asked Rodney pointedly.

"Why of course I don't want you to have bad luck."

"Thank you. You are very considerate."

"Suppose you lose your place, shall you go back to selling papers?"

"I hope to find something better to do."

"Where are you going now?"

"To get some lunch."

"So am I. Suppose we go together."

"Very well, provide you will lunch with me."

"I don't want to impose upon you."

"You won't. We may not meet again for some time, and we shall have this meal to remind us of each other."

They went to a well known restaurant on Park Row. Rodney ordered a liberal dinner for himself, and Jasper followed his example nothing loath. He was always ready to dine at the expense of others, but even as he ate he could not help wondering at the strange chance that had made him the guest of a boy who was selling papers the day before.

He had nearly finished eating when a disturbing thought occurred to him. Suppose Rodney didn't have money enough to settle the bill, and threw it upon him.

When Rodney took the checks and walked up to the cashier's desk he followed him with some anxiety. But his companion quietly took out a five dollar bill, from his pocket, and tendered it to the cashier. The latter gave him back the right change and the two boys went out into the street.

"You seem to have plenty of money," said Jasper.

"There are very few who would admit having that," smiled Rodney.

"I don't see why you sold papers if you have five dollar bills in your pocket."

"I don't want to be idle."

"May I tell my uncle and Mr. Goodnow that you have got a place?"

"If you like."

"Well, good by, I must be hurrying back to the store."

Rodney smiled. He rather enjoyed Jasper's surprise and perplexity.

CHAPTER XVIII.
RODNEY'S SECRET IS DISCOVERED.

Jasper lost no time in acquainting his uncle with Rodney's extraordinary good fortune. James Redwood was surprised, but not all together incredulous.

"I don't understand it," he said, "but Ropes appears to be a boy of truth. Perhaps he may have exaggerated the amount of his salary."

"I hardly think so, uncle. He gave me a tip top dinner down on Park Row."

"He may have been in funds from selling the articles taken from the store."

"That's so!" assented Jasper, who had the best possible reason for knowing that it was not so.

"I wish the boy well," said his uncle. "He always treated me respectfully, and I never had anything against him except the loss of stock, and it is not certain that he is the thief."

"I guess there isn't any doubt about that."

"Yet, believing him to be a thief, you did not hesitate to accept a dinner from him."

"I didn't want to hurt his feelings," replied Jasper, rather sheepishly.

"Do you know what sort of a place he has got, or with what house?"

"No; he wouldn't tell me."

"He thought perhaps you would inform the new firm of the circumstances under which he left us. I don't blame him, but I am surprised that he should have been engaged without a recommendation."

"Shall you tell Mr. Goodnow?"

"Not unless he asks about Ropes. I don't want to interfere with the boy in any way."

In the store, as has already been stated, Jasper succeeded to Rodney's place, and in consequence his pay was raised to seven dollars a week. Still it was not equal to what it had been when he was receiving additional money from the sale of the articles stolen by Philip Carton and himself.

The way in which they had operated was this: Philip would come in and buy a cloak or a dress pattern from Jasper, and the young salesman would pack up two or three instead of one. There was a drawback to the profit in those cases, as Carton would be obliged to sell both at a reduced price. Still they had made a considerable sum from these transactions, though not nearly as much as Mr. Goodnow had lost.

After the discovery of the thefts and the discharge of Rodney, the two confederates felt that it would be imprudent to do any more in that line. This suspension entailed heavier loss on Carton than on Jasper. The latter had a fixed income and a home at his uncle's house, while Philip had no regular income, though he occasionally secured a little temporary employment.

In the meantime Rodney had commenced his tutorship. His young pupil became very fond of him, and being a studious boy, made rapid progress in his lessons.

Mr. Sargent felt that his experiment, rash as it might be considered, vindicated his wisdom by its success. At the end of a month he voluntarily raised Rodney's salary to twenty dollars a week.

"I am afraid you are overpaying me, Mr. Sargent," said Rodney.

"That's my lookout. Good service is worth a good salary, and I am perfectly satisfied with you."

"Thank you, sir. I prize that even more than the higher salary."

Only a portion of Rodney's time was spent in teaching. In the afternoon he and his charge went on little excursions, generally to Central Park.

One holiday, about four months after the commencement of Rodney's engagements, he was walking in the Park when he fell in with Jasper. Jasper's attention was at once drawn to the little boy, whose dress and general appearance indicated that he belonged to a wealthy family. This excited Jasper's curiosity.

"How are you, Rodney?" said Jasper adroitly. "It is a good while since I met you."

"Yes."

"Who is the little boy with you?"

"His name is Arthur Sargent."

Rodney gave this information unwillingly, for he saw that his secret was likely to be discovered.

"How do you do, Arthur?" asked Jasper, with unwonted affability, for he did not care for children.

"Pretty well," answered Arthur politely.

"Have you known Rodney long?"

"Why, he is my teacher," answered Arthur in some surprise.

Jasper's eyes gleamed with sudden intelligence. So this was Rodney's secret, and this was the position for which he was so well paid.

Rodney bit his lip in vexation, but made no remark.

"Does he ever punish you for not getting your lessons?" asked Jasper without much tact.

"Of course not," answered Arthur indignantly.

"Arthur always does get his lessons," said Rodney. "I suppose you have a holiday from work today, Jasper."

"Yes; I am glad to get away now and then."

"I must bid you good morning now."

"Won't you let me call on you? Where do you live, Arthur?"

The boy gave the number of his house.

Jasper asked Arthur, thinking rightly that he would be more likely to get an answer from him than from Rodney. He walked away triumphantly, feeling that he had made a discovery that might prove of advantage to him.

"Is that a friend of yours, Rodney?" asked little Arthur.

"I have known him for some time."

"I don't like him very much."

"Why?" asked Rodney with some curiosity.

"I don't know," answered the little boy slowly. "I can't like everybody."

"Quite true, Arthur. Jasper is not a special friend of mine, and I am not particular about your liking him. I hope you like me."

"You know I do, Rodney," and he gave Rodney's hand an assuring pressure.

Ten minutes after he left Rodney, Jasper fell in with Carton. The intimacy between them had perceptibly fallen off. It had grown out of business considerations.

Now that it was no longer safe to abstract articles from the store, Jasper felt that he had no more use for his late confederate. When they met he treated him with marked coldness.

On this particular day Carton was looking quite shabby. In fact, his best suit was in pawn, and he had fallen back on one half worn and soiled.

"Hello!" exclaimed Jasper, and was about to pass on with a cool nod.

"Stop!" said Philip, looking offended.

"I am in a hurry," returned Jasper. "I can't stop today."

"You are in a hurry, and on a holiday?"

"Yes; I am to meet a friend near the lake."

"I'll go along with you."

Jasper had to submit, though with an ill grace.

"Wouldn't another day do?"

"No; the fact is, Jasper, I am in trouble."

"You usually are," sneered Jasper.

"That is so. I have been out of luck lately."

"I am sorry, but I can't help it as I see."

"How much money do you think I have in my pockets?"

"I don't know, I am sure. I am not good at guessing conundrums."

"Just ten cents."

"That isn't much," said Jasper, indifferently.

"Let me have a dollar, that's a good fellow!"

"You seem to think I am made of money," said Jasper sharply. "I haven't got much more myself."

"Then you might have. You get a good salary."

"Only seven dollars."

"You are able to keep most of it for yourself."

"Suppose I am? You seem to know a good deal of my affairs."

"Haven't you any pity for an old friend?"

"Yes, I'll give you all the pity you want, but when it comes to money it's a different matter. Here you are, a man of twenty six, ten years older than me, and yet you expect me to help support you."

"You didn't use to talk to me like that."

"Well, I do now. You didn't use to try to get money out of me."

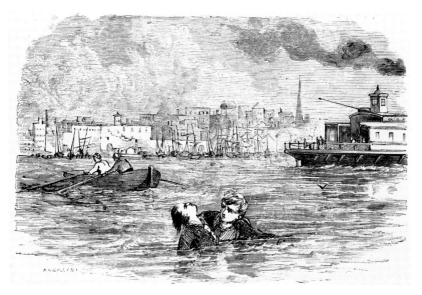

9. Ragged Dick, quick to act while everyone else gasped in terror, leaps into the East River to rescue a lad who fell from deck of the Brooklyn ferry. From *Ragged Dick*.

10. A dramatic rescue in *Hector's Inheritance*. The hero, driven from home and deprived of his legacy by a scheming uncle, saves a little girl from being "crushed beneath the hoofs of the horses and the wheels of the carriage."

12. Horatio Alger, Jr., as he appeared in the *Argosy* for Saturday, December 22, 1888.

11. With a few belongings tied in a handkerchief, many of Alger's heroes left the farm to seek their fortune in the city. They lived clean and—with luck and pluck—prospered, returning in time to pay off the mortgage and save the old homestead from clutches of villainous squire.

13. "Smash your baggage, mam?" says the hero of Alger's *Ben the Luggage Boy.*

14. In *Brave and Bold*, as in a number of Alger tales, the hero finds himself shipwrecked. But the deserted island sometimes concealed a treasure and, when rescued by a passing vessel, he resumes his homeward journey, a wealthy young man.

15. At conclusion of *Sink or Swim*, Harry Raymond—back from Australia with newly won riches—settles a debt with the villainous Squire Turner. "Foiled at all points," Alger joyously concluded, "he dashed his hat angrily upon his head, and rushed from the house in undignified haste."

16. A typical cover page from *Argosy*, the magazine that serialized many Alger novels.

17. Illustrated title page from *The Western Boy*, which appeared only briefly before being reissued as *Tom the Bootblack*, title under which it became one of the author's most popular stories. The hero, a youth "of enterprising disposition," tells customer he is "ready to adopt a rich father." Alger used "western" to describe such areas as Chicago, Milwaukee and Cincinnati. Beyond lay Indian Territory and the vast Pacific wilderness.

18. Treatment accorded to the typical Alger hero by the typical Alger villain.

"Look here, Jasper! I am poor, but I don't want you to talk to me as you are doing."

"Indeed!" sneered Jasper.

"And I won't have it," said Carton firmly. "Listen to me, and I will propose a plan that will help us both."

"What is it?"

"You can easily secrete articles, if you are cautious, without attracting notice, and I will dispose of them and share the money with you."

Jasper shook his head.

"I wouldn't dare to do it," he said. "Somebody might spy on me."

"Not if you are careful."

"If it were found out I would be bounced like Ropes."

"What is he doing? Have you seen him lately?"

"He is getting on finely. He is earning fifteen dollars a week."

"You don't mean it?"

"Yes I do."

"What firm is he working for?"

"For none at all. He is tutor to a young kid."

"I didn't know he was scholar enough."

"Oh yes, he knows Greek and Latin and a lot of other stuff."

"Who is the boy?"

"I don't feel at liberty to tell. I don't think he would care to have you know."

"I'll tell you what you can do. Borrow five dollars of him for me."

"I don't know about that. If I were to borrow it would be for myself."

"You can do as you please. If you don't do something for me I will write to Mr. Goodnow that you are the thief who stole the cloaks and dress patterns."

"You wouldn't do that?" exclaimed Jasper in consternation.

"Wouldn't I? I am desperate enough to do anything."

After a little further conference Jasper agreed to do what was asked of him. He did not dare to refuse.

CHAPTER XIX.
JASPER'S REVENGE.

Rodney was considerably surprised one evening to receive a call from Jasper in his room. He was alone, as Mike had been detailed about a week ago for night duty. The room looked more attractive than formerly. Rodney had bought a writing desk, which stood in the corner, and had put up three pictures, which, though cheap, were attractive.

"Good evening, Jasper," he said. "It is quite friendly of you to call."

"I hadn't anything else on hand this evening, and thought I would come round see how you were getting along."

"Take a seat and make yourself at home."

"Do you object to cigarettes?" asked Jasper, producing one from a case in his pocket.

"I object to smoking them myself, but I don't want to dictate to my friends."

"You look quite comfortable here," continued Jasper in a patronizing tone.

"We try to be comfortable, though our room is not luxurious."

"Who do you mean by 'we'? Have you a room mate?"

"Yes. Mike Flynn rooms with me."

"Who is he—a newsboy?"

"No. He is a telegraph boy."

"You don't seem to very particular," said Jasper, shrugging his shoulders.

"I am very particular."

"Yet you room with an Irish telegraph boy."

"He is a nice boy of good habits, and a devoted friend. What could I want more?"

"Oh, well, you have a right to consult your own taste."

"You have a nice home, no doubt."

"I live with my uncle. Yes, he has a good house, but I am not so independent as if I had a room outside."

"How are things going on at the store?"

"About the same as usual. Why don't you come in some day?"

"For two reasons; I am occupied during the day, and I don't want to go where I am considered a thief."

"I wish I was getting your income. It is hard to get along on seven dollars a week."

"Still you have a nice home, and I suppose you have most of your salary to yourself."

"Yes, but there isn't much margin in seven dollars. My uncle expects me to buy my own clothes. You were lucky to get out of the store. Old Goodnow ought to give me ten dollars."

"Don't let him hear you speak of him as *old* Goodnow, Jasper."

"Oh, I'm smart enough for that. I mean to keep on the right side of the old chap. What sort of a man are you working for?"

"Mr. Sargent is a fine man."

"He isn't mean certainly. I should like to be in your shoes."

"If I hear of any similar position shall I mention your name?" asked Rodney, smiling.

"No; I could not take care of a kid. I hate them."

"Still Arthur is a nice boy."

"You are welcome to him. What do you have to teach?"

"He is studying Latin and French, besides English branches."

"I know about as much of Latin and French as a cow. I couldn't be a teacher. I say, Rodney," and Jasper cleared his throat, "I want you to do me a favor."

"What is it?"

"I want you to lend me ten dollars."

Rodney was not mean, but he knew very well that a loan to Jasper would be a permanent one. Had Jasper been his friend even this consideration would not have inspired a refusal, but he knew very well that Jasper had not a particle of regard for him.

"I don't think I can oblige you, Jasper," he said.

"Why not? You get fifteen dollars a week."

"My expenses are considerable. Besides I am helping Mike, whose salary is very small. I pay the whole of the rent, and I have paid for some clothes for him."

"You are spending your money very foolishly," said Jasper frowning.

"Would I spend it any less foolishly if I should lend you ten dollars?"

"There is some difference between Mike Flynn and me. I am a gentleman."

"So is Mike."

"A queer sort of gentleman! He is only a poor telegraph boy."

"Still he is a gentleman."

"I should think you might have money enough for both of us."

"I might, but I want to save something from my salary. I don't know how long I shall be earning as much. I might lose my place."

"So you might."

"And I could hardly expect to get another where the pay would be as good."

"I would pay you on installments—a dollar a week," urged Jasper.

"I don't see how you could, as you say your pay is too small for you now."

"Oh, well, I could manage."

"I am afraid I can't oblige you, Jasper," said Rodney in a decided tone.

"I didn't think you were so miserly," answered Jasper in vexation.

"You may call it so, if you like. You must remember that I am not situated like you. You have your uncle to fall back upon in case you lose your position, but I have no one. I have to hustle for myself."

"Oh, you needn't make any more excuses. I suppose ten dollars is rather a large sum to lend. Can you lend me five?"

"I am sorry, but I must refuse you."

Jasper rose from the chair on which he had been sitting.

"Then I may as well go," he said. "I am disappointed in you, Ropes. I thought you were a good, whole souled fellow, and not a miser."

"You must think of me as you please, Jasper. I feel that I have a right to regulate my own affairs."

"All I have to say is this, if you lose your place as you may very soon, don't come round to the store and expect to be taken back."

"I won't," answered Rodney, smiling. "I wouldn't go back at any rate unless the charge of theft was withdrawn."

"That will never be!"

"Let it be so, as long as I am innocent."

Jasper left the room abruptly, not even having the politeness to bid Rodney good evening.

Rodney felt that he was quite justified in refusing to lend Jasper money. Had he been in need he would have obliged him, though he had no reason to look upon him as a friend.

No one who knew Rodney could regard him as mean or miserly. Could he have read Jasper's thoughts as he left the house he would have felt even less regret at disappointing him.

About two days afterward when Rodney went up to meet his pupil, Mr. Sargent handed him a letter.

"Here is something that concerns you, Rodney," he said. "It doesn't appear to be from a friend of yours."

With some curiosity Rodney took the letter and read it.

It ran thus:

Mr. John Sargent:

Dear Sir—I think it my duty to write and tell you something about your son's tutor—something that will surprise and shock you. Before he entered your house he was employed by a firm on Reade Street. He was quite a favorite with his employer, Mr. Otis Goodnow, who promoted him in a short time. All at once it was found that articles were missing from the stock. Of course it was evident that some one of the clerks was dishonest. A watch was set, and finally it was found that Rodney Ropes had taken the articles, and one—a lady's cloak—was found in his room by a detective. He was discharged at once without a recommendation.

For a time he lived by selling papers, but at last he managed to get into your house. I am sure you won't regard him as fit to educate your little son, though I have no doubt he is a good scholar. But his character is bad— I don't think he ought to have concealed this from you out of friendship for you, and because I think it is my duty, I take the liberty of writing. If you doubt this I will refer to Mr. Goodnow, or Mr. James Redwood, who had charge of the room in which Ropes was employed.

Yours very respectfully,

A FRIEND.

"You knew all this before, Mr. Sargent," said Rodney, as he handed back the letter.

"Yes. Have you any idea who wrote it?"

"I feel quite sure that it was a boy about two years older than myself, Jasper Redwood."

"Is he related to the man of the same name whom he mentions?"

"Yes, he is his nephew."

"Has he any particular reason for disliking you, Rodney?"

"Yes, sir. He came round to my room Wednesday evening, and asked me to lend him ten dollars."

"I presume you refused."

"Yes, sir. He is not in need. He succeeded to my place, and he has a home at the house of his uncle."

"He appears to be a very mean boy. Anonymous letters are always cowardly, and generally malicious. This seems to be no exception to the general rule."

"I hope it won't affect your feelings towards me, Mr. Sargent."

"Don't trouble yourself about that, Rodney. I am not so easily prejudiced against one of whom I have a good opinion."

"I suppose this is Jasper's revenge," thought Rodney.

Jasper had little doubt that his letter would lead to Rodney's loss of position. It was certainly a mean thing to plot another's downfall, but Jasper was quite capable of it. Had he secured the loan he asked he would have been willing to leave Rodney alone, but it would only have been the first of a series of similar applications.

It was several days before Jasper had an opportunity of learning whether his malicious plan had succeeded or not. On Sunday forenoon he met Rodney on Fifth Avenue just as the church services were over. He crossed the street and accosted the boy he had tried to injure.

"Good morning, Ropes," he said, examining Rodney's face curiously to see whether it indicated trouble of any kind.

"Good morning!" responded Rodney coolly.

"How are you getting along in your place?"

"Very well, thank you."

"Shall I find you at your pupil's house if I call there some afternoon?"

"Yes, unless I am out walking with Arthur."

"I wonder whether he's bluffing," thought Jasper. "I daresay he wouldn't tell me if he had been discharged. He takes it pretty coolly."

"How long do you think your engagement will last?" he asked.

"I don't know. I never had a talk with Mr. Sargent on that point."

"Do you still give satisfaction?"

Rodney penetrated Jasper's motives for asking all these questions, and was amused.

"I presume if I fail to satisfy Mr. Sargent he will tell me so."

"It would be a nice thing if you could stay there three or four years."

"Yes: but I don't anticipate it. When Arthur gets a little older he will be sent to school."

"What will you do then?"

"I haven't got so far as that."

"I can't get anything out of him," said Jasper to himself. "I shouldn't be a bit surprised if he were already discharged."

They had now reached Madison Square, and Jasper left Rodney.

The latter looked after him with a smile.

"I think I have puzzled Jasper," he said to himself. "He was anxious to know how his scheme had worked. He will have to wait a little longer."

"If Mr. Sargent keeps Ropes after my letter he must be a fool," Jasper decided. "I wonder if Ropes handles the mail. He might have suppressed the letter."

But Rodney was not familiar with his handwriting, and would have no reason to suspect that the particular letter contained anything likely to injure him in the eyes of Mr. Sargent.

Later in his walk Jasper met Philip Carton. His former friend was sitting on a bench in Madison Square. He called out to Jasper as he passed.

"Come here, Jasper, I want to talk with you."

Jasper looked at him in a manner far from friendly.

"I am in a hurry," he said.

"What hurry can you be in? Come and sit down here. I *must* speak to you."

Jasper did not like his tone, but it impressed him, and he did not dare to refuse.

He seated himself beside Philip, but looked at him askance. Carton was undeniably shabby. He had the look of a man who was going down hill and that rapidly.

"I shall be late for dinner," grumbled Jasper.

"I wish I had any dinner to look forward to," said Carton. "Do you see this money?" and he produced a nickel from his pocket.

"What is there remarkable about it?"

"It is the last money I have. It won't buy me a dinner."

"I am sorry, but it is none of my business," said Jasper coolly. "You are old enough to attend to your own affairs."

"And I once thought you were my friend," murmured Philip bitterly.

"Yes, we were friends in a way."

"Now you are up and I am down— Jasper, I want a dollar."

"I dare say you do. Plenty want that."

"I want it from you."

"I can't spare it."

"You can spare it better than you can spare your situation."

"What do you mean by that?" asked Jasper, growing nervous.

"I'll tell you what I mean. How long do you think you would stay in the store if Mr. Goodnow knew that you were concerned in the thefts from which he has suffered?"

"Was I the only one?"

"No; I am equally guilty."

"I am glad you acknowledge it. You see you had better keep quiet for your own sake."

"If I keep quiet I shall starve."

"Do you want to go to prison?"

"I shouldn't mind so much if you went along, too."

"Are you crazy, Philip Carton?"

"No, I am not, but I am beginning to get sensible. If I go to prison I shall at least have enough to eat, and now I haven't."

"What do you mean by all this foolish talk?"

"I mean that if you won't give me any money I will go to the store and tell Mr. Goodnow something that will surprise him."

Jasper was getting thoroughly frightened.

"Come, Philip," he said, "listen to reason. You know how poor I am."

"No doubt. I know you have a good home and enough to eat."

"I only get seven dollars a week."

"And I get nothing."

"I have already been trying to help you. I went to Ropes the other day, and asked him to lend me five dollars. I meant it for you."

"Did he give it to you?"

"He wouldn't give me a cent. He is mean and miserly!"

"I don't know. He knows very well that you are no friend of his, though he doesn't know how much harm you have done him."

"He's rolling in money. However, I've put a spoke in his wheel, I hope."

"How?"

"I wrote an anonymous letter to Mr. Sargent telling him that Ropes was discharged from the store on suspicion of theft."

"You are a precious scamp, Jasper."

"What do you mean?"

"You are not content with getting Ropes discharged for something which you yourself did——"

"And you too."

"And I too. I accept the amendment. Not content with that, you try to get him discharged from his present position."

"Then he might have lent me the money," said Jasper sullenly.

"It wouldn't have been a loan. It would have been a gift. But no matter about that. I want a dollar."

"I can't give it to you."

"Then I shall call at the store tomorrow morning and tell Mr. Goodnow about the stolen goods."

Finding that Carton was in earnest, Jasper finally, but with great reluctance, drew out a dollar and handed it to his companion.

"There, I hope that will satisfy you," he said spitefully.

"It will—for the present."

"I wish he'd get run over or something," thought Jasper. "He seems to expect me to support him, and that on seven dollars a week."

Fortunately for Jasper, Philip Carton obtained employment the next day which lasted for some time, and as he was paid ten dollars a week he was not under the necessity of troubling his old confederate for loans.

Now and then Jasper and Rodney met, but there were no cordial relations between them. Jasper could not forgive Rodney for refusing to lend him money, and Rodney was not likely to forget the anonymous letter by which Jasper had tried to injure him.

So three months passed. One day Mr. Sargent arrived at home before it was time for Rodney to leave.

"I am glad to see you, Rodney," said his employer. "I have some news for you which I am afraid will not be entirely satisfactory to you."

"What is it, sir?"

"For the last three years I have been wishing to go to Europe with my wife and Arthur. The plan has been delayed, because I could not make satisfactory business arrangements. Now, however, that difficulty has been overcome, and I propose to sail in about two weeks."

"I hope you'll enjoy your trip, sir."

"Thank you. Of course it will terminate, for a time at least, your engagement to teach Arthur."

"I shall be sorry for that, sir, but I am not selfish enough to want you to stay at home on that account."

"I thought you would feel that way. I wish I could procure you another position before I go, but that is uncertain. I shall, however, pay you a month's salary in advance in lieu of a notice."

"That is very liberal, sir."

"I think it only just. I have been very well pleased with your attention to Arthur, and I know he has profited by your instructions as well as enjoyed your companionship. I hope you have been able to save something."

"Yes, sir, I have something in the Union Dime Savings Bank."

"That's well. You will remain with me one week longer, but the last week Arthur will need for preparations."

Two weeks later Rodney stood on the pier and watched the stately Etruria steam out into the river. Arthur and his father were on deck, and the little boy waved his handkerchief to his tutor as long as he could see him.

Rodney turned away sadly.

"I have lost a good situation," he soliloquized. "When shall I get another?"

CHAPTER XXI.
CONTINUED ILL LUCK.

Rodney set himself to work searching for a new situation. But wherever he called he found some one ahead of him. At length he saw an advertisement for an entry clerk in a whole-sale house in Church Street. He applied and had the good fortune to please the superintendent.

"Where have you worked before?" he asked.

"At Otis Goodnow's, on Reade Street."

"How much were you paid there?"

"Seven dollars a week."

"Very well, we will start you on that salary, and see if you earn it."

Rodney was surprised and relieved to find that he was not asked for a recommendation from Mr. Goodnow, knowing that he could not obtain one. He went to work on a Monday morning, and found his duties congenial and satisfactory.

Seven dollars a week was small, compared with what he had received as a tutor, but he had about two hundred and fifty dollars in the Union Dime Savings Bank and drew three dollars from this fund every week in order that he might still assist Mike, whose earnings were small.

One of his new acquaintances in the store was James Hicks, a boy about a year older than himself.

"Didn't you use to work at Otis Goodnow's?" asked James one day when they were going to lunch.

"Yes."

"I know a boy employed there. He is older than either of us."

"Who is it?"

"Jasper Redwood. Of course you know him."

"Yes," answered Rodney with a presentiment of evil.

He felt that it would be dangerous to have Jasper know of his present position, but did not venture to give a hint of this to James.

His fears were not groundless. Only the day after James met Jasper on the street.

"Anything new?" asked Jasper.

"Yes; we've got one of your old friends in our store."

"Who is it?"

"Rodney Ropes."

Jasper stopped short, and whistled. He was excessively surprised, as he supposed Rodney still to be Arthur Sargent's tutor.

"You don't mean it?" he ejaculated.

"Why not? Is there anything so strange about it?"

"Yes. Did Ropes bring a recommendation from Mr. Goodnow?"

"I suppose so. I don't know."

"If he did, it's forged."

"Why should it be?"

"Goodnow wouldn't give him a recommendation."

"Why wouldn't he?"

"Because he discharged Ropes. Do you want to know why?"

"Yes."

"For stealing articles from the store."

It was the turn of James Hicks to be surprised.

"I can't believe it," he said.

"It's true. Just mention the matter to Ropes, and you'll see he won't deny it."

"I think there must be some mistake about it. Rodney doesn't look like a fellow that would steal."

"Oh, you can't tell from appearances— Rogues are always plausible."

"Still mistakes are sometimes made. I'd trust Rodney Ropes sooner than any boy I know."

"You don't know him as well as I do."

"You don't like him?" said James shrewdly.

"No I don't. I can't like a thief."

"You talk as if you had a grudge against him."

"Nothing but his being a thief. Well, what are you going to do about it?"

"About what?"

"What I have just told you."

"I don't feel that I have any call to do anything."

"You ought to tell your employer."

"I am no telltale," said James scornfully.

"Then you will let him stay in the store, knowing him to be a thief?"

"I don't know him to be a thief. If he steals anything it will probably be found out."

Jasper urged James to give information about Rodney, but he steadily refused.

"I leave others to do such dirty work," he said, "and I don't think any better of you, let me tell you, for your eagerness to turn the boy out of his position."

"You are a queer boy."

"Think so if you like," retorted Hicks. "I might give my opinion of you."

At this point Jasper thought it best to let the conversation drop. He was much pleased to learn that Rodney had lost his fine position as tutor, and was now in a place from which he might more easily be ousted.

As he could not prevail upon James Hicks to betray Rodney he decided to write an anonymous letter to the firm that employed him.

The result was that the next afternoon Rodney was summoned to the office.

"Sit down Ropes," said the superintendent. "For what store did you work before you came into our house?"

"Otis Goodnow's."

"Under what circumstances did you leave?"

"I was accused of theft."

"You did not mention this matter when you applied for a situation here."

"No, sir. I ought perhaps to have done so, but I presumed in that case you would not have given me a place."

"You are right, he would not."

"Nor would I have applied had the charge been a true one. Articles were certainly missing from Mr. Goodnow's stock, but in accusing me they did me a great injustice."

"How long since you left Mr. Goodnow's?"

"Four months."

"What have you been doing since?"

"I was acting as tutor to the son of Mr. Sargent, of West Fifty Eighth Street."

"A well known citizen. Then you are a scholar?"

"Yes, sir, I am nearly prepared for college."

"Of course he did not know you were suspected of dishonesty."

"On the contrary he did know it. I told him, and later he received an anonymous letter, notifying him of the fact."

"We also have received an anonymous letter. Here it is. Do you recognize the hand writing?"

"Yes," answered Rodney after examining the letter. "It was written by Jasper Redwood."

"Who is he?"

"A boy employed by Mr. Goodnow. For some reason he seems to have a spite against me."

"I admit that it is pretty small business to write an anonymous letter calculated to injure another. Still we shall have to take notice of this."

"Yes, sir, I suppose so."

"I shall have to bring it to the notice of the firm. What they may do I don't know. If the matter was to be decided by me I would let you stay."

"Thank you, sir," said Rodney gratefully.

"But I am not Mr. Hall. You can go now and I will see you again."

Rodney left the office fully persuaded that his engagement would speedily terminate. He was right; the next day he was sent for again.

"I am sorry to tell you, Ropes," said the superintendent kindly "that Mr. Hall insists upon your being discharged. He is a nervous man and rather suspicious. I spoke in your favor but I could not turn him."

"At any rate I am grateful to you for your friendly efforts."

The superintendent hesitated a moment, and then said: "Will this discharge seriously embarrass you? Are you short of money?"

"No, sir. I was very liberally paid by Mr. Sargent, and I saved money. I have enough in the savings bank to last me several months, should I be idle so long."

"I am glad of it. I hope you will remember, my boy, that this is none of my doings. I would gladly retain you. I will say one thing more, should Jasper Redwood ever apply for a situation here, his name will not be considered."

So Rodney found himself again without a position. It seemed hard in view of his innocence, but he had confidence to believe that something would turn up for him as before. At any rate he had enough money to live on for some time.

When Mike Flynn learned the circumstances of his discharge he was very angry.

"I'd like to meet Jasper Redwood," he said, his eyes flashing. "If I didn't give him a laying out, then my name isn't Mike Flynn."

"I think he will get his deserts some time, Mickey, without any help from you or me."

"Should hope he will. And what'll you do now, Rodney?"

"I don't know. Sometimes I think it would be well to go to some other city, Boston or Philadelphia, where Jasper can't get on my track."

"Should hope you won't do it. I can't get along widout you."

"I will stay here for a few weeks, Mike, and see if anything turns up."

"I might get you in as a telegraph boy."

"That wouldn't suit me. It doesn't pay enough."

Rodney began to hunt for a situation again, but four weeks passed and brought him no success. One afternoon about four o'clock he was walking up Broadway when, feeling tired, he stepped into the Continental Hotel at the corner of Twentieth Street.

He took a seat at some distance back from the door, and in a desultory way began to look about him. All at once he started in surprise, for in a man sitting in one of the front row of chairs he recognized Louis Wheeler, the railroad thief who had stolen his box of jewelry.

Wheeler was conversing with a man with a large flapping

sombrero, and whose dress and general appearance indicated that he was a Westerner.

Rodney left his seat, and going forward sat down in the chair behind Wheeler. He suspected that the Western man was in danger of being victimized.

CHAPTER XXII.

AN OLD ACQUAINTANCE TURNS UP.

In his new position Rodney could easily hear the conversation which took place between the Western man and his old railroad acquaintance.

"I am quite a man of leisure," said Wheeler, "and it will give me great pleasure to go about with you and show you our city."

"You are very obliging."

"Oh, don't mention it. I shall really be glad to have my time occupied. You see I am a man of means—my father left me a fortune—and so I am not engaged in any business."

"You are in luck. I was brought up on a farm in Vermont, and had to borrow money to take me to Montana four years ago."

"I hope you prospered in your new home?"

"I did. I picked up twenty five thousand dollars at the mines, and doubled it by investment in lots in Helena."

"Very neat, indeed. I inherited a fortune from my father—a hundred and twenty five thousand dollars—but I never made a cent myself. I don't know whether I am smart enough."

"Come out to Montana and I'll put you in a way of making some money."

"Really, now, that suggestion strikes me favorably. I believe I will follow your advice. When shall you return to your Western home?"

"In about a fortnight, I think."

"You must go to the theater tonight. There is a good play on at the Madison Square."

"I don't mind. When can I get tickets?"

"I'll go and secure some. It is only a few blocks away."

"Do so. How much are the tickets?"

"A dollar and a half or two dollars each."

"Here are five dollars, if it won't trouble you too much."

"My dear friend, I meant to pay for the tickets. However, I will pay next time. If you will remain here I will be back in twenty minutes."

Louis Wheeler left the hotel with the five dollars tucked away in his vest pocket.

He had no sooner disappeared than Rodney went forward and occupied his seat.

"Excuse me, sir," he said to the miner, "but do you know much of the man who has just left you?"

"I only met him here. He seems a good natured fellow. What of him?"

"He said he was a man of independent means."

"Isn't he?"

"He is a thief and an adventurer."

The miner was instantly on the alert.

"How do you know this?" he asked.

"Because he stole a box of jewelry from me in the cars some months ago."

"Did you get it again?"

"Yes; he left the train, but I followed him up and reclaimed the jewelry."

"Was it of much value?"

"They were family jewels, and were worth over a thousand dollars."

"Do you think he wants to bunco me?"

"I have no doubt of it."

"I have given him money to buy theater tickets. Do you think he will come back?"

"Yes. He wouldn't be satisfied with that small sum."

"Tell me about your adventure with him."

"I will do it later. The theater is so near that he might come back and surprise us together. I think he would recognize me."

"Do you advise me to go to the theater?"

"Yes, but be on your guard."

"Where can I see you again?"

"Are you staying at this hotel?"

"Yes. Here is my card."

Rodney read this name on the card:

JEFFERSON PETTIGREW.

"I wish you were going to the theater with us."

"It wouldn't do. Mr. Wheeler would remember me."

"Then come round and breakfast with me tomorrow—at eight o'clock, sharp."

"I will, sir. Now I will take a back seat, and leave you to receive your friend."

"Don't call him my friend. He seems to be a mean scoundrel."

"Don't let him suspect anything from your manner."

"I won't. I want to see him expose his plans."

Five minutes afterwards Louis Wheeler entered the hotel.

"I've got the tickets," he said, "but I had to buy them of a speculator, and they cost me more than I expected."

"How much?"

"Two and a half apiece. So there is no change coming back to you."

"Never mind! As long as you had enough money to pay for them it is all right."

As a matter of fact Wheeler bought the tickets at the box office at one dollar and fifty cents each, which left him a profit of two dollars. When he saw how easily the Western man took it he regretted not having represented that the tickets cost three dollars each.

However, he decided that there would be other ways of plundering his new acquaintance. He took his seat again next to the miner.

"It is not very late," he said. "Would you like a run out to Central Park or to Grant's Tomb?"

"Not today. I feel rather tired. By the way, you did not mention your name."

"I haven't a card with me, but my name is Louis Wheeler."

"Where do you live, Mr. Wheeler?"

"I am staying with an aunt on Fifth Avenue, but I think of taking board at the Windsor Hotel. It is a very high toned house, and quite a number of my friends board there."

"Is it an expensive hotel?"

"Oh, yes, but my income is large and——"

"I understand. Now, Mr. Wheeler, I must excuse myself, as I feel tired. Come at half past seven and we can start for the theater together."

"Very well."

Wheeler rose reluctantly, for he had intended to secure a dinner from his new acquaintance, but he was wise enough to take the hint.

After he left the room Rodney again joined Mr. Pettigrew.

"He didn't give me back any change," said the Western man. "He said he bought the tickets of a speculator at two dollars and a half each."

"Then he made two dollars out of you."

"I suppose that is the beginning. Well, that doesn't worry me. But I should like to know how he expects to get more money out of me. I don't understand the ways of this gentry."

"Nor I very well. If you are on your guard I think you won't be in any danger."

"I will remember what you say. You seem young to act as adviser to a man like me. Are you in business?"

"At present I am out of work, but I have money enough to last me three months."

"Are you, like my new acquaintance, possessed of independent means?"

"Not now, but I was six months ago."

"How did you lose your money?"

"I did not lose it. My guardian lost it for me."

"What is your name?"

"Rodney Ropes."

"You've had some pretty bad luck. Come up to my room and tell me about it."

"I shall be glad to do so, sir."

Mr. Pettigrew called for his key and led the way up to a plain room on the third floor.

"Come in," he said. "The room is small, but I guess it will hold us both. Now go ahead with your story."

In a short time Rodney had told his story in full to his new acquaintance, encouraged to do so by his sympathetic manner. Mr. Pettigrew was quite indignant, when told of Jasper's mean and treacherous conduct.

"That boy Jasper is a snake in the grass," he said. "I'd like to give him a good thrashing."

"There isn't any love lost between us, Mr. Pettigrew, but I think it will turn out right in the end. Still I find it hard to get a place in New York with him circulating stories about me."

"Then why do you stay in New York?"

"I have thought it might be better to go to Philadelphia or Boston."

"I can tell you of a better place than either."

"What is that?"

"Montana."

"Do you really think it would be wise for me to go there?"

"Think? I haven't a doubt about it."

"I have money enough to get there, but not much more. I should soon have to find work, or I might get stranded."

"Come back with me, and I'll see you through. I'll make a bargain with you. Go round with me here, and I'll pay your fare out to Montana."

"If you are really in earnest I will do so, and thank you for the offer."

"Jefferson Pettigrew means what he says. I'll see you through, Rodney."

"But I may be interfering with your other friend, Louis Wheeler."

"I shall soon be through with him. You needn't worry yourself about that."

Mr. Pettigrew insisted upon Rodney's taking supper with him. Fifteen minutes after Rodney left him Mr. Wheeler made his appearance.

CHAPTER XXIII.
MR. WHEELER HAS A SET BACK.

Louis Wheeler had not seen Rodney in the hotel office, and probably would not have recognized him if he had, as Rodney was quite differently dressed from the time of their first meeting. He had no reason to suppose, therefore, that Mr. Pettigrew had been enlightened as to his real character.

It was therefore with his usual confidence that he accosted his acquaintance from Montana after supper.

"It is time to go to the theater, Mr. Pettigrew," he said.

Jefferson Pettigrew scanned his new acquaintance with interest. He had never before met a man of his type and he looked upon him as a curiosity.

He was shrewd, however, and did not propose to let Wheeler know that he understood his character. He resolved for the present to play the part of the bluff and unsuspecting country visitor.

"You are very kind, Mr. Wheeler," he said, "to take so much trouble for a stranger."

"My dear sir," said Wheeler effusively, "I wouldn't do it for many persons, but I have taken a fancy to you."

"You don't mean so?" said Pettigrew, appearing pleased.

"Yes, I do, on my honor."

"But I don't see why you should. You are a polished city gentleman and I am an ignorant miner from Montana."

Louis Wheeler looked complacent when he was referred to as a polished city gentleman.

"You do yourself injustice, my dear Pettigrew," he said in a patronizing manner. "You do indeed. You may not be polished, but you are certainly smart, as you have shown by accumulating a fortune."

"But I am not as rich as you."

"Perhaps not, but if I should lose my money, I could not make another fortune, while I am sure you could. Don't you think it would be a good plan for us to start a business together in New York?"

"Would you really be willing to go into business with me?"

Jefferson Pettigrew asked this question with so much apparent sincerity that Wheeler was completely deceived.

"I've got him dead!" he soliloquized complacently.

He hooked his arm affectionately in the Montana miner's and said, "My dear friend, I have never met a man with whom I would rather be associated in business than with you. How much capital could you contribute?"

"I will think it over, Mr. Wheeler. By the way what business do you propose that we shall go into?"

"I will think it over and report to you."

By this time they had reached the theater. The play soon commenced. Mr. Pettigrew enjoyed it highly, for he had not had much opportunity at the West of attending a high class theatrical performance.

When the play ended, Louis Wheeler said, "Suppose we go to Delmonico's and have a little refreshment."

"Very well."

They adjourned to the well known restaurant, and Mr. Pettigrew ordered an ice and some cakes, but his companion made a hearty supper. When the bill came, Louis Wheeler let it lie on the table, but Mr. Pettigrew did not appear to see it.

"I wonder if he expects me to pay for it," Wheeler asked himself anxiously.

"Thank you for this pleasant little supper," said Pettigrew mischievously. "Delmonico's is certainly a fine place."

Wheeler changed color. He glanced at the check. It was for two dollars and seventy five cents, and this represented a larger sum than he possessed.

He took the check and led the way to the cashier's desk. Then he examined his pockets.

"By Jove," he said, "I left my wallet in my other coat. May I borrow five dollars till tomorrow?"

Jefferson Pettigrew eyed him shrewdly. "Never mind," he said, "I will pay the check."

"I am very much ashamed of having put you to this expense."

"If that is all you have to be ashamed of Mr. Wheeler," said the miner pointedly, "you can rest easy."

"What do you mean?" stammered Wheeler.

"Wait till we get into the street, and I will tell you."

They went out at the Broadway entrance, and then Mr. Pettigrew turned to his new acquaintance.

"I think I will bid you good night and good by at the same time, Mr. Wheeler," he said.

"My dear sir, I hoped you won't misjudge me on account of my unfortunately leaving my money at home."

"I only wish to tell you that I have not been taken in by your plausible statements, Mr. Wheeler, if that is really your name. Before we started for the theater I had gauged you and taken your measure."

"Sir, I hope you don't mean to insult me!" blustered Wheeler.

"Not at all. You have been mistaken in me, but I am not

mistaken in you. I judge you to be a gentlemanly adventurer, ready to take advantage of any who have money and are foolish enough to be gulled by your tricks. You are welcome to the profit you made out of the theater tickets, also to the little supper to which you have done so much justice. I must request you, now, however, to devote yourself to some one else, as I do not care to meet you again."

Louis Wheeler slunk away, deciding that he had made a great mistake in setting down his Montana acquaintance as an easy victim.

"I didn't think he'd get on to my little game so quick," he reflected. "He's sharper than he looks."

Rodney took breakfast with Mr. Pettigrew the next morning. When breakfast was over, the Montana man said:

"I'm going to make a proposal to you, Rodney. How much pay did you get at your last place?"

"Seven dollars a week."

"I'll pay you that and give you your meals. In return I want you to keep me company and go about with me."

"I shall not be apt to refuse such an offer as that, Mr. Pettigrew, but are you sure you prefer me to Mr. Wheeler?" laughed Rodney.

"Wheeler be—blessed!" returned the miner.

"How long are you going to stay in New York?"

"About two weeks. Then I shall go back to Montana and take you with me."

"Thank you. There is nothing I should like better."

Two days later, as the two were walking along Broadway, they met Mr. Wheeler. The latter instantly recognized his friend from Montana, and scrutinized closely his young companion.

Rodney's face looked strangely familiar to him, but somehow he could not recollect when or under what circumstances he had met him. He did not, however, like to give up his intended victim, but had the effrontery to address the man from Montana.

"I hope you are well, Mr. Pettigrew."

"Thank you, I am very well."

"I hope you are enjoying yourself. I should be glad to show you the sights. Have you been to Grant's Tomb?"

"Not yet."

"I should like to take you there."

"Thank you, but I have a competent guide."

"Won't you introduce me to the young gentleman?"

"I don't require any introduction to you, Mr. Wheeler," said Rodney.

"Where have I met you before?" asked Wheeler abruptly.

"In the cars. I had a box of jewelry with me," answered Rodney significantly.

Louis Wheeler changed color. Now he remembered Rodney, and he was satisfied that he owed to him the coolness with which the Western man had treated him.

"I remember you had," he said spitefully, "but I don't know how you came by it."

"It isn't necessary that you should know. I remember I had considerable difficulty in getting it out of your hands."

"Mr. Pettigrew," said Wheeler angrily, "I feel interested in you, and I want to warn you against the boy who is with you. He is a dangerous companion."

"I dare say you are right," said Pettigrew in a quizzical tone. "I shall look after him sharply, and I thank you for your kind and considerate warning. I don't care to take up any more of your valuable time. Rodney, let us be going."

"It must have been the kid that exposed me," muttered Wheeler, as he watched the two go down the street. "I will get even with him some time. That man would have been good for a thousand dollars to me if I had not been interfered with."

"You have been warned against me, Mr. Pettigrew," said

Rodney, laughing. "Mr. Wheeler has really been very unkind in interfering with my plans."

"I shan't borrow any trouble, or lie awake nights thinking about it, Rodney. I don't care to see or think of that rascal again."

The week passed, and the arrangement between Mr. Pettigrew and Rodney continued to their mutual satisfaction. One morning, when Rodney came to the Continental as usual, his new friend said: "I received a letter last evening from my old home in Vermont."

"I hope it contained good news."

"On the contrary it contained bad news. My parents are dead, but I have an old uncle and aunt living. When I left Burton he was comfortably fixed, with a small farm of his own, and two thousand dollars in bank. Now I hear that he is in trouble. He has lost money, and a knavish neighbor has threatened to foreclose a mortgage on the farm and turn out the old people to die or go to the poorhouse."

"Is the mortgage a large one?"

"It is much less than the value of the farm, but ready money is scarce in the town, and that old Sheldon calculates upon. Now I think of going to Burton to look up the matter."

"You must save your uncle, if you can, Mr. Pettigrew."

"I can and I will. I shall start for Boston this afternoon by the Fall River boat and I want you to go with me."

"I should enjoy the journey, Mr. Pettigrew."

"Then it is settled. Go home and pack your gripsack. You may be gone three or four days."

CHAPTER XXIV.
A CHANGE OF SCENE.

"Now," said Mr. Pettigrew, when they were sitting side by side on the upper deck of the Puritan, the magnificent steamer on the Fall River line. "I want you to consent to a little plan that will mystify my old friends and neighbors."

"What is it, Mr. Pettigrew?"

"I have never written home about my good fortune; so far as they know I am no better off than when I went away."

"I don't think I could have concealed my success."

"It may seem strange, but I'll explain—I want to learn who are my friends and who are not. I am afraid I wasn't very highly thought of when I left Burton. I was considered rather shiftless.

"I was always in for a good time, and never saved a cent. Everybody predicted that I would fail, and I expect most wanted me to fail. There were two or three, including my uncle, aunt and the friend who lent me money, who wished me well.

"I mustn't forget to mention the old minister who baptized me when I was an infant. The good old man has been preaching thirty or forty years on a salary of four hundred dollars, and has had to run a small farm to make both ends meet. He believed in me and gave me good advice. Outside of these I don't remember any one who felt an interest in Jefferson Pettigrew."

"You will have the satisfaction of letting them see that they did not do you justice."

"Yes, but I may not tell them—that is none except my true friends. If I did, they would hover round me and want to borrow money, or get me to take them out West with me. So I have hit upon a plan. I shall want to use money, but I will pretend it is yours."

Rodney opened his eyes in surprise.

"I will pass you off as a rich friend from New York, who feels an interest in me and is willing to help me."

Rodney smiled.

"I don't know if I can look the character," he said.

"Oh yes you can. You are nicely dressed, while I am hardly any better dressed than when I left Burton."

"I have wondered why you didn't buy some new clothes when you were able to afford it."

"You see we Western miners don't care much for style, perhaps not enough. Still I probably shall buy a suit or two, but not till I have made my visit home. I want to see how people will receive me, when they think I haven't got much money. I shall own up to about five hundred dollars, but that isn't enough to dazzle people even in a small country village."

"I am willing to help you in any way you wish, Mr. Pettigrew."

"Then I think we shall get some amusement out of it. I shall represent you as worth about a hundred thousand dollars."

"I wish I were."

"Very likely you will be some time if you go out to Montana with me."

"How large a place is Burton?"

"It has not quite a thousand inhabitants. It is set among the hills, and has but one rich man, Lemuel Sheldon, who is worth perhaps fifty thousand dollars, but puts on the airs of a millionaire."

"You are as rich as he, then."

"Yes, and shall soon be richer. However, I don't want him to know it. It is he who holds the mortgage on my uncle's farm."

"Do you know how large the mortgage is?"

"It is twelve hundred dollars. I shall borrow the money of you to pay it."

"I understand," said Rodney, smiling.

"I shall enjoy the way the old man will look down upon me very much as a millionaire looks down upon a town pauper."

"How will he look upon me?"

"He will be very polite to you, for he will think you richer than himself."

"On the whole, we are going to act a comedy, Mr. Pettigrew. What is the name of the man who lent you money to go to Montana?"

"A young carpenter, Frank Dobson. He lent me a hundred dollars, which was about all the money he had saved up."

"He was a true friend."

"You are right. He was. Everybody told Frank that he would never see his money again, but he did. As soon as I could get together enough to repay him I sent it on, though I remember it left me with less than ten dollars in my pocket.

"I couldn't bear to think that Frank would lose anything by me. You see we were chums at school and always stood by each other. He is married and has two children."

"While you are an old bachelor."

"Yes; I ain't in a hurry to travel in double harness. I'll wait till I am ready to leave Montana, with money enough to live handsomely at home."

"You have got enough now."

"But I may as well get more. I am only thirty years old, and I can afford to work a few years longer."

"I wish I could be sure of being worth fifty thousand dollars when I am your age."

"You have been worth that, you tell me."

"Yes, but I should value more money that I had made my-self."

Above five o'clock on Monday afternoon Mr. Pettigrew and Rodney reached Burton. It was a small village about four miles from the nearest railway station. An old fashioned Concord stage connected Burton with the railway. The driver was on the platform looking out for passengers when Jefferson Pettigrew stepped out of the car.

"How are you, Hector?" said the miner, in an off hand way.

"Why, bless my soul if it isn't Jeff!" exclaimed the driver, who had been an old schoolmate of Mr. Pettigrew's.

"I reckon it is," said the miner, his face lighting up with the satisfaction he felt at seeing a home face.

"Why, you ain't changed a mite, Jeff. You look just as you did when you went away. How long have you been gone?"

"Four years!"

"Made a fortune? But you don't look like it. That's the same suit you wore when you went away, isn't it?"

Mr. Pettigrew laughed.

"Well no, it isn't the same, but it's one of the same kind."

"I thought maybe you'd come home in a dress suit."

"It isn't so easy to make a fortune, Hector."

"But you have made something, ain't you?"

"Oh, yes, when I went away I hadn't a cent except what I borrowed. Now I've got five hundred dollars."

"That ain't much."

"No, but it's better than nothing. How much more have you got, Hector?"

"Well, you see I married last year. I haven't had a chance to lay by."

"So you see I did as well as if I had stayed at home."

"Are you going to stay home now?"

"For a little while. I may go back to Montana after a bit."

"Is it a good place to make money?"

"I made five hundred dollars."

"That's only a little more than a hundred dollars a year. Frank Dobson has saved as much as that, and he's stayed right here in Burton."

"I'm glad of that," said Pettigrew heartily. "Frank is a rousing good fellow. If it hadn't been for him I couldn't have gone to Montana."

"It doesn't seem to have done you much good, as I can see."

"Oh, well, I am satisfied. Let me introduce my friend, Mr. Rodney Ropes of New York."

"Glad to meet you," said Hector with a jerk of the head.

"Rodney, won't you sit inside? I want to sit outside with Hector."

"All right, Mr. Pettigrew."

"Who is that boy?" asked Hector with characteristic Yankee curiosity, as he seized the lines and started the horses.

"A rich young fellow from New York. I got acquainted with him there."

"Rich is he?"

Jefferson Pettigrew nodded.

"How rich do you think?"

"Shouldn't wonder if he might be worth a hundred thousand."

"You don't say! Why, he beats Squire Sheldon."

"Oh, yes, Squire Sheldon wouldn't be considered rich in New York."

"How did he get his money?"

"His father left him a fortune."

"Is that so? I wish my father had left me a fortune."

"He did, didn't he?"

"Yes, he did! When his estate was settled I got seventy five dollars, if you call that a fortune. But I say, what brings the boy to Burton?"

"His friendship for me, I expect. Besides he may invest in a place."

"There's the old Morse place for sale. Do you think he'd buy that?"

"It wouldn't be nice enough for him. I don't know any place that would be good enough except the squire's."

"The squire wouldn't sell."

"Oh, well, I don't know as Rodney would care to locate in Burton."

"You're in luck to get such a friend. Say, do you think he would lend you a hundred dollars if you were hard up?"

"I know he would. By the way, Hector, is there any news? How is my uncle?"

"I think the old man is worrying on account of his mortgage."

"Who holds it?"

"The squire. They do say he is goin' to foreclose. That'll be bad for the old man. It'll nigh about break his heart, I expect."

"Can't uncle raise the money to pay him?"

"Who is there round here who has got any money except the squire?"

"That's so."

"Where are you goin' to stop, Jeff?"

"I guess I'll stop at the tavern tonight, but I'll go over and call on uncle this evening."

CHAPTER XXV.

JEFFERSON PETTIGREW'S HOME.

News spreads fast in a country village. Scarcely an hour had passed when it was generally known that Jefferson Pettigrew had come home from Montana with a few hundred dollars in money, bringing with him a rich boy who could buy out all Burton. At least that is the way the report ran.

When the two new arrivals had finished supper and come out on the hotel veranda there were a dozen of Jefferson Pettigrew's friends ready to welcome him.

"How are you, Jefferson, old boy?" said one and another.

"Pretty well, thank you. It seems good to be home."

"I hear you've brought back some money."

"Yes, a few hundred dollars."

"That's better than nothing. I reckon you'll stay home now."

"I can't afford it, boys."

"Are ye goin' back to Montany?"

"Yes. I know the country, and I can make a middlin' good livin' there."

"I say, is that boy that's with you as rich as they say?"

"I don't know what they say."

"They say he's worth a million."

"Oh no, not so much as that. He's pretty well fixed."

"Hasn't he got a father livin'?"

"No, it's his father that left the money."

"How did you happen to get in with him?"

"Oh, we met promiscuous. He took a sort of fancy to me, and that's the way of it."

"Do you expect to keep him with you?"

"He talks of goin' back to Montana with me. I'll be sort of guardian to him."

"You're in luck, Jeff."

"Yes, I'm in luck to have pleasant company. Maybe we'll join together and buy a mine."

"Would you mind introducin' him?"

"Not at all," and thus Rodney became acquainted with quite a number of the Burton young men. He was amused to see with what deference they treated him, but preserved a sober face and treated all cordially, so that he made a favorable impression on those he met.

Among those who made it in their way to call on the two travelers was Lemuel Sheldon, the rich man of the village.

"How do you do, Jefferson?" he said condescendingly.

"Very well, sir."

"You have been quite a traveler."

"Yes, sir; I have been to the far West."

"And met with some success, I am told."

"Yes, sir; I raised money enough to get home."

"I hear you brought home a few hundred dollars."

"Yes, sir."

"Oh, well," said the squire patronizingly, "that's a good beginning."

"It must seem very little to a rich man like you, squire."

"Oh, no!" said the squire patronizingly. "You are a young man. I shouldn't wonder if by the time you get as old as I am you might be worth five thousand dollars."

"I hope so," answered Mr. Pettigrew demurely.

"By the way, you have brought a young man with you, I am told."

"Yes."

"I should like to make his acquaintance. He is rich, is he not?"

"I wish I was as rich."

"You don't say so! About how much do you estimate he is worth?"

"I don't think it amounts to quite as much as a quarter of a million. Still, you know it is not always easy to tell how much a person is worth."

"He is certainly a *very* fortunate young man," said the squire, impressed. "What is his name?"

"Rodney Ropes."

"The name sounds aristocratic. I shall be glad to know him."

"Rodney," said Mr. Pettigrew. "I want to introduce you to Squire Sheldon, our richest and most prominent citizen."

"I am glad to meet you, Squire Sheldon," said Rodney, offering his hand.

"I quite reciprocate the feeling, Mr. Ropes, but Mr. Pettigrew should not call me a rich man. I am worth something, to be sure."

"I should say you were, squire," said Jefferson. "Rodney, he is as rich as you are."

"Oh no," returned the squire, modestly, "not as rich as that. Indeed, I hardly know how much I am worth. As Mr. Pettigrew very justly observed it is not easy to gauge a man's possessions. But there is one difference between us. You, Mr. Ropes, I take it, are not over eighteen."

"Only sixteen, sir."

"And yet you are wealthy. I am rising fifty. When you come to my age you will be worth much more."

"Perhaps I may have lost all I now possess," said Rodney. "Within a year I have lost fifty thousand dollars."

"You don't say so."

"Yes; it was through a man who had charge of my property. I think now I shall manage my money matters myself."

"Doubtless you are right. That was certainly a heavy loss. I shouldn't like to lose so much. I suppose, however, you had something left?"

"Oh yes," answered Rodney in an indifferent tone.

"He must be rich to make so little account of fifty thousand dollars," thought the squire.

"How long do you propose to stay in town, Mr. Pettigrew?" he asked.

"I can't tell, sir, but I don't think I can spare more than three or four days."

"May I hope that you and Mr. Ropes will take supper with me tomorrow evening?"

"Say the next day and we'll come. Tomorrow I must go to my uncle's."

"Oh very well!"

Squire Sheldon privately resolved to pump Rodney as to the investment of his property. He was curious to learn first how much the boy was worth, for if there was anything that the squire worshiped it was wealth. He was glad to find that Mr. Pettigrew had only brought home five hundred dollars, as it was not enough to lift the mortgage on his uncle's farm.

After they were left alone Jefferson Pettigrew turned to Rodney and said, "Do you mind my leaving you a short time and calling at my uncle's?"

"Not at all, Mr. Pettigrew. I can pass my time very well."

Jefferson Pettigrew directed his steps to an old fashioned farmhouse about half a mile from the village. In the rear the roof sloped down so that the eaves were only five feet from the ground. The house was large though the rooms were few in number.

In the sitting room sat an old man and his wife, who was

nearly as old. It was not a picture of cheerful old age, for each looked sad. The sadness of old age is pathetic for there is an absence of hope, and courage, such as younger people are apt to feel even when they are weighed down by trouble.

Cyrus Hooper was seventy one, his wife two years younger. During the greater part of their lives they had been well to do, if not prosperous, but now their money was gone, and there was a mortgage on the old home which they could not pay.

"I don't know what's goin' to become of us, Nancy," said Cyrus Hooper. "We'll have to leave the old home, and when the farm's been sold there won't be much left over and above the mortgage which Louis Sheldon holds."

"Don't you think the squire will give you a little more time, Cyrus?"

"No; I saw him yesterday, and he's sot on buyin' in the farm for himself. He reckons it won't fetch more'n eighteen hundred dollars."

"That's only six hundred over the mortgage."

"It isn't that, Nancy. There's about a hundred dollars due in interest. We won't get more'n five hundred dollars."

"Surely, Cyrus, the farm is worth three thousand dollars."

"So it is, Nancy, but that won't do us any good, as long as no one wants it more'n the squire."

"I wish Jefferson were at home."

"What good would it do? I surmise he hasn't made any money. He never did have much enterprise, that boy."

"He was allus a good boy, Cyrus."

"That's so, Nancy, but he didn't seem cut out for makin' money. Still it would do me good to see him. Maybe we might have a home together, and manage to live."

Just then a neighbor entered.

"Have you heard the news?" she asked.

"No; what is it?"

"Your nephew Jefferson Pettigrew has got back."

"You don't mean so. There, Jefferson, that's one comfort."

"And they say he has brought home five hundred dollars."

"That's more'n I thought he'd bring. Where is he?"

"Over at the tavern. He's brought a young man with him, leastways a boy, that's got a lot of money."

"The boy?"

"Yes; he's from New York, and is a friend of Jefferson's."

"Well, I'm glad he's back. Why didn't he come here?"

"It's likely he would if the boy wasn't with him."

"Perhaps he heard of my misfortune."

"I hope it'll all come right, Mr. Hooper. My, if there ain't Jefferson comin' to see you now. I see him through the winder. I guess I'll be goin'. You'll want to see him alone."

CHAPTER XXVI.

THE BOY CAPITALIST.

"How are you, Uncle Cyrus?" said Jefferson Pettigrew heartily, as he clasped his uncle's toil worn hand. "And Aunt Nancy, too! It pays me for coming all the way from Montana just to see you."

"I'm glad to see you, Jefferson," said his uncle. "It seems a long time since you went away. I hope you've prospered."

"Well, uncle, I've brought myself back well and hearty, and I've got a few hundred dollars."

"I'm glad to hear it, Jefferson. You're better off than when you went away."

"Yes, uncle. I couldn't be much worse off. Then I hadn't a cent that I could call my own. But how are you and Aunt Nancy?"

"We're gettin' old, Jefferson, and misfortune has come to us. Squire Sheldon has got a mortgage on the farm and it's likely we'll be turned out. You've come just in time to see it."

"Is it so bad as that, Uncle Cyrus? Why, when I went away you were prosperous."

"Yes, Jefferson, I owned the farm clear, and I had money in the bank, but now the money's gone and there's a twelve hundred dollar mortgage on the old place," and the old man sighed.

"But how did it come about, uncle? You and Aunt Nancy haven't lived extravagantly, have you? Aunt Nancy, you haven't run up a big bill at the milliner's and dressmaker's?"

"You was always for jokin', Jefferson," said the old lady, smiling faintly; "but that is not the way our losses came."

"How then?"

"You see I indorsed notes for Sam Sherman over at Canton, and he failed, and I had to pay. Then I bought some wild cat minin' stock on Sam's recommendation, and that went down to nothin'. So between the two I lost about three thousand dollars. I've been a fool, Jefferson, and it would have been money in my pocket if I'd had a guardeen."

"So you mortgaged the place to Squire Sheldon, uncle?"

"Yes; I had to. I was obliged to meet my notes."

"But surely the squire will extend the mortgage."

"No, he won't. I've asked him. He says he must call in the money, and so the old place will have to be sold, and Nancy and I must turn out in our old age."

Again the old man sighed, and tears came into Nancy Hooper's eyes.

"There'll be something left, won't there, Uncle Cyrus?"

"Yes, the place should bring six hundred dollars over and above the mortgage. That's little enough, for it's worth three thousand."

"So it is, Uncle Cyrus. But what can you do with six hundred dollars? It won't support you and Aunt Nancy?"

"I thought mebbe, Jefferson, I could hire a small house and you could board with us, so that we could still have a home together."

"I'll think it over, uncle, if there is no other way. But are you sure Squire Sheldon won't give you more time?"

"No, Jefferson. I surmise he wants the place himself. There's talk of a railroad from Sherborn, and that'll raise the price of land right around here. It'll probably go right through the farm just south of the three acre lot."

"I see, Uncle Cyrus. You ought to have the benefit of the rise in value."

"Yes, Jefferson, it would probably rise enough to pay off the mortgage, but it's no use thinkin' of it. The old farm has got to go."

"I don't know about that, Uncle Cyrus."

"Why, Jefferson, you haven't money enough to lift the mortgage!" said the old man, with faint hope.

"If I haven't I may get it for you. Tell me just how much money is required."

"Thirteen hundred dollars, includin' interest."

"Perhaps you have heard that I have a boy with me—a boy from New York, named Rodney Ropes. He has money, and perhaps I might get him to advance the sum you want."

"Oh, Jefferson, if you only could!" exclaimed Aunt Nancy, clasping her thin hands. "It would make us very happy."

"I'll see Rodney tonight and come over tomorrow morning and tell you what he says. On account of the railroad I shall tell him that it is a good investment. I suppose you will be willing to mortgage the farm to him for the same money that he pays to lift the present mortgage?"

"Yes, Jefferson, I'll be willin' and glad. It'll lift a great burden from my shoulders. I've been worryin' at the sorrow I've brought upon poor Nancy, for she had nothing to do with my foolish actions. I was old enough to know better, Jefferson, and I'm ashamed of what I did."

"Well, Uncle Cyrus, I'll do what I can for you. Now let us forget all about your troubles and talk over the village news. You know I've been away for four years, and I haven't had any stiddy correspondence, so a good deal must have happened that

I don't know anything about. I hear Frank Dobson has prospered?"

"Yes, Frank's pretty forehanded. He's got a good economical wife, and they've laid away five or six hundred dollars in the savings bank."

"I am glad of it. Frank is a good fellow. If it hadn't been for him I couldn't have gone to Montana. When he lent me the money everybody said he'd lose it, but I was bound to pay it if I had to live on one meal a day. He was the only man in town who believed in me at that time."

"You was a littless shif'less, Jefferson. You can't blame people. I wasn't quite sure myself how you'd get along."

"No doubt you are right, Uncle Cyrus. It did me good to leave town. I didn't drink, but I had no ambition. When a man goes to a new country it's apt to make a new man of him. That was the case with me."

"Are you goin' back again, Jefferson?"

"Yes, uncle. I'm going to stay round here long enough to fix up your affairs and get you out of your trouble. Then I'll go back to the West. I have a little mining interest there and I can make more money there than I can here."

"If you can get me out of my trouble, Jefferson, I'll never forget it. Nancy and I have been so worried that we couldn't sleep nights, but now I'm beginnin' to be a little more cheerful."

Jefferson Pettigrew spent another hour at his uncle's house, and then went back to the tavern, where he found Rodney waiting for him. He explained briefly the part he wished his boy friend to take in his plan for relieving his uncle.

"I shall be receiving credit to which I am not entitled," said Rodney. "Still, if it will oblige you I am willing to play the part of the boy capitalist."

The next morning after breakfast the two friends walked over to the house of Cyrus Hooper. Aunt Nancy came to the door and gave them a cordial welcome.

"Cyrus is over at the barn, Jefferson," she said. "I'll ring the bell and he'll come in."

"No, Aunt Nancy, I'll go out and let him know I am here."

Presently Cyrus Hooper came in, accompanied by Jefferson.

"Uncle Cyrus," said the miner, "let me introduce you to my friend Rodney Ropes, of New York."

"I'm glad to see you," said Cyrus heartily. "I'm glad to see any friend of Jefferson's."

"Thank you, sir. I am pleased to meet you."

"Jefferson says you are goin' to Montany with him."

"I hope to do so. I am sure I shall enjoy myself in his company."

"How far is Montany, Jefferson?"

"It is over two thousand miles away, Uncle Cyrus."

"It must be almost at the end of the world. I don't see how you can feel at home so far away from Vermont."

Jefferson smiled.

"I can content myself wherever I can make a good living," he said. "Wouldn't you like to go out and make me a visit?"

"No, Jefferson, I should feel that it was temptin' Providence to go so far at my age."

"You never were very far from Burton, Uncle Cyrus?"

"I went to Montpelier once," answered the old man with evident pride. "It is a nice sizable place. I stopped at the tavern, and had a good time."

It was the only journey the old man had ever made, and he would never forget it.

"Uncle Cyrus," said Jefferson, "this is the young man who I thought might advance you money on a new mortgage. Suppose we invite him to go over the farm, and take a look at it so as to see what he thinks of the investment."

"Sartain, Jefferson, sartain! I do hope Mr. Ropes you'll look favorable on the investment. It is Jefferson's idea, but it would be doin' me a great favor."

"Mr. Pettigrew will explain the advantages of the farm as we go along," said Rodney.

So they walked from field to field, Jefferson expatiating to his young friend upon the merits of the investment, Rodney asking questions now and then to carry out his part of the shrewd and careful boy capitalist.

When they had made a tour of the farm Jefferson said: "Well, Rodney, what do you think of the investment?"

"I am satisfied with it," answered Rodney. "Mr. Hooper, I will advance you the money on the conditions mentioned by my friend, Mr. Pettigrew."

Tears of joy came into the eyes of Cyrus Hooper and his worn face showed relief.

"I am very grateful, young man," he said. "I will see that you don't regret your kindness."

"When will Squire Sheldon be over to settle matters, Uncle Cyrus?" asked Jefferson.

"He is comin' this afternoon at two o'clock."

"Then Rodney and I will be over to take part in the business."

CHAPTER XXVII.
THE FAILURE OF SQUIRE SHELDON'S
PLOT.

On the morning of the same day Squire Sheldon sat in his study when the servant came in and brought a card.

"It's a gentleman that's come to see you, sir," she said.

Lemuel Sheldon's eye brightened when he saw the name, for it was that of a railroad man who was interested in the proposed road from Sherborn.

"I am glad to see you, Mr. Caldwell," he said cordially, rising to receive his guest. "What is the prospect as regards the railroad?"

"I look upon it as a certainty," answered Enoch Caldwell, a grave, portly man of fifty.

"And it is sure to pass through our town?"

"Yes, I look upon that as definitely decided."

"The next question is as to the route it will take," went on the squire. "Upon that point I should like to offer a few suggestions."

"I shall be glad to receive them. In fact, I may say that my report will probably be accepted, and I shall be glad to consult you."

"Thank you. I appreciate the compliment you pay me, and, though I say it, I don't think you could find any one more thoroughly conversant with the lay of the land and the most advisable route to follow. If you will put on your hat we will go out together and I will give you my views."

"I shall be glad to do so."

The two gentlemen took a leisurely walk through the village, going by Cyrus Hooper's house on the way.

"In my view," said the squire, "the road should go directly through this farm a little to the north of the house."

The squire proceeded to explain his reasons for the route he recommended.

"To whom does the farm belong?" asked Caldwell, with a shrewd glance at the squire.

"To an old man named Cyrus Hooper."

"Ahem! Perhaps he would be opposed to the road passing so near his house."

"I apprehend that he will not have to be consulted," said the squire with a crafty smile.

"Why not?"

"Because I hold a mortgage on the farm which I propose to foreclose this afternoon."

"I see. So that you will be considerably benefited by the road."

"Yes, to a moderate extent."

"But if a different course should be selected, how then?"

"If the road goes through the farm I would be willing to give a quarter of the damages awarded to me to—you understand?"

"I think I do. After all it seems the most natural route."

"I think there can be no doubt on that point. Of course the corporation will be willing to pay a reasonable sum for land taken."

"I think I can promise that, as I shall have an important voice in the matter."

"I see you are a thorough business man," said the squire. "I hold that it is always best to pursue a liberal policy."

"Quite so. You have no doubt of obtaining the farm?"

"Not the slightest."

"But suppose the present owner meets the mortgage?"

"He can't. He is a poor man, and he has no moneyed friends.
I confess I was a little afraid that a nephew of his just returned
from Montana might be able to help him, but I learn that he
has only brought home five hundred dollars while the mortgage, including interest, calls for thirteen hundred."

"Then you appear to be safe. When did you say the matter
would be settled?"

"This afternoon at two o'clock. You had better stay over and
take supper with me. I shall be prepared to talk with you at
that time."

"Very well."

From a window of the farmhouse Cyrus Hooper saw Squire
Sheldon and his guest walking by the farm, and noticed the interest which they seemed to feel in it. But for the assurance
which he had received of help to pay the mortgage he would
have felt despondent, for he guessed the subject of their conversation. As it was, he felt an excusable satisfaction in the certain defeat of the squire's hopes of gain.

"It seems that the more a man has the more he wants, Jefferson," he said to his nephew. "The squire is a rich man—the
richest man in Burton—but he wants to take from me the little property that I have."

"It's the way of the world, Uncle Cyrus. In this case the
squire is safe to be disappointed, thanks to my young friend,
Rodney."

"It's lucky for me, Jefferson, that you came home just the
time you did. If you had come a week later it would have been
too late."

"Then you don't think the squire would have relented?"

"I know he wouldn't. I went over a short time since and had

a talk with him on the subject. I found he was sot on gettin' the
farm into his own hands."

"If he were willing to pay a fair value it wouldn't be so bad."

"He wasn't. He wanted to get it as cheap as he could."

"I wonder," said Jefferson Pettigrew reflectively, "whether I
shall be as hard and selfish if ever I get rich."

"I don't believe you will, Jefferson. I don't believe you will.
It doesn't run in the blood."

"I hope not, Uncle Cyrus. How long have you known the
squire?"

"Forty years, Jefferson. He is about ten years younger than I
am. I was a young man when he was a boy."

"And you attend the same church?"

"Yes."

"And still he is willing to take advantage of you and reduce
you to poverty. I don't see much religion in that."

"When a man's interest is concerned religion has to stand
to one side with some people."

It was in a pleasant frame of mind that Squire Sheldon left
his house and walked over to the farmhouse which he hoped to
own. He had decided to offer eighteen hundred dollars for the
farm, which would be five hundred over and above the face of
the mortgage with the interest added.

This of itself would give him an excellent profit, but he expected also, as we know, to drive a stiff bargain with the new
railroad company, for such land as they would require to use.

"Stay here till I come back, Mr. Caldwell," he said. "I apprehend it won't take me long to get through my business."

Squire Sheldon knocked at the door of the farmhouse, which
was opened to him by Nancy Hooper.

"Walk in, squire," she said.

"Is your husband at home, Mrs. Hooper?"

"Yes; he is waiting for you."

Mrs. Hooper led the way into the sitting room, where her husband was sitting in a rocking chair.

"Good afternoon, Mr. Hooper," said the squire. "I hope I see you well."

"As well as I expect to be. I'm gettin' to be an old man."

"We must all grow old," said the squire vaguely.

"And sometimes a man's latter years are his most sorrowful years."

"That means that he can't pay the mortgage," thought Squire Sheldon.

"Well, ahem! Yes, it does sometimes happen so," he said aloud.

"Still if a man's friends stand by him, that brings him some comfort."

"I suppose you know what I've come about, Mr. Hooper," said the squire, anxious to bring his business to a conclusion.

"I suppose it's about the mortgage."

"Yes, it's about the mortgage."

"Will you be willing to extend it another year?"

"I thought," said the squire, frowning, "I had given you to understand that I cannot do this. You owe me a large sum in accrued interest."

"But if I make shift to pay this?"

"I should say the same. It may as well come first as last. You can't hold the place, and there is no chance of your being better off by waiting."

"I understand that the new railroad might go through my farm. That would put me on my feet."

"There is no certainty that the road will ever be built. Even if it were, it would not be likely to cross your farm."

"I see, Squire Sheldon, you are bound to have the place."

"There is no need to put it that way, Mr. Hooper. I lent you money on mortgage. You can't pay the mortgage, and of course I foreclose. However, I will buy the farm and allow you eighteen hundred dollars for it. That will give you five hundred dollars over and above the money you owe me."

"The farm is worth three thousand dollars."

"Nonsense, Mr. Hooper. Still if you get an offer of that sum *today* I will advise you to sell."

"I certainly won't take eighteen hundred."

"You won't? Then I shall foreclose, and you may have to take less."

"Then there is only one thing to do."

"As you say, there is only one thing to do."

"And that is, to pay off the mortgage and clear the farm."

"You can't do it!" exclaimed the squire uneasily.

Cyrus Hooper's only answer was to call "Jefferson."

Jefferson Pettigrew entered the room, followed by Rodney.

"What does this mean?" asked the squire.

"It means, Squire Sheldon," said Mr. Pettigrew, "that you won't turn my uncle out of his farm this time. My young friend, Rodney Ropes, has advanced Uncle Cyrus money enough to pay off the mortgage."

"I won't take a check," said the squire hastily.

"You would have to if we insisted upon it, but I have the money here in bills. Give me a release and surrender the mortgage, and you shall have your money."

It was with a crestfallen look that Squire Sheldon left the farmhouse, though his pockets were full of money.

"It's all up," he said to his friend Caldwell in a hollow voice. "They have paid the mortgage."

After all the railway did cross the farm, and Uncle Cyrus was paid two thousand dollars for the right of way, much to the disappointment of his disinterested friend Lemuel Sheldon, who felt that this sum ought to have gone into his own pocket.

CHAPTER XXVIII.

A MINISTER'S GOOD FORTUNE.

"I have another call to make, Rodney," said Mr. Pettigrew, as they were on their way back to the hotel, "and I want you to go with me."

"I shall be glad to accompany you anywhere, Mr. Pettigrew."

"You remember I told you of the old minister whose church I attended as a boy. He has never received but four hundred dollars a year, yet he has managed to rear a family, but has been obliged to use the strictest economy."

"Yes, I remember."

"I am going to call on him, and I shall take the opportunity to make him a handsome present. It will surprise him, and I think it will be the first present of any size that he has received in his pastorate of over forty years.

"There he lives!" continued Jefferson, pointing out a very modest cottage on the left hand side of the road.

It needed painting badly, but it looked quite as well as the minister who came to the door in a ragged dressing gown. He was venerable looking, for his hair was quite white, though he was only sixty five years old. But worldly cares which had come upon him from the difficulty of getting along on his scanty salary had whitened his hair and deepened the wrinkles on his kindly face.

"I am glad to see you, Jefferson," he said, his face lighting up with pleasure. "I heard you were in town and I hoped you wouldn't fail to call upon me."

"I was sure to call, for you were always a good friend to me as well as many others."

"I always looked upon you as one of my boys, Jefferson. I hear that you have been doing well."

"Yes, Mr. Canfield. I have done better than I have let people know."

"Have you been to see your uncle? Poor man, he is in trouble."

"He is no longer in trouble. The mortgage is paid off, and as far as Squire Sheldon is concerned he is independent."

"Indeed, that is good news," said the old minister with beaming face. "You must surely have done well if you could furnish money enough to clear the farm. It was over a thousand dollars, wasn't it?"

"Yes, thirteen hundred. My young friend, Rodney Ropes, and myself managed it between us."

"I am glad to see you, Mr. Ropes. Come in both of you. Mrs. Canfield will be glad to welcome you."

They followed him into the sitting room, the floor of which was covered by an old and faded carpet. The furniture was of the plainest description. But it looked pleasant and homelike, and the papers and books that were scattered about made it more attractive to a visitor than many showy city drawing rooms.

"And how are all your children, Mr. Canfield?" asked Jefferson.

"Maria is married to a worthy young man in the next town. Benjamin is employed in a book store, and Austin wants to

go to college, but I don't see any way to send him, poor boy!"
and the minister sighed softly.

"Does it cost much to keep a boy in college?"

"Not so much as might be supposed. There are beneficiary
funds for deserving students, and then there is teaching to eke
out a poor young man's income, so that I don't think it would
cost over a hundred and fifty dollars a year."

"That isn't a large sum."

"Not in itself, but you know, Jefferson, my salary is only four
hundred dollars a year. It would take nearly half my income, so
I think Austin will have to give up his hopes of going to college and follow in his brother's steps."

"How old is Austin now?"

"He is eighteen."

"Is he ready for college?"

"Yes, he could enter at the next commencement but for the
financial problem."

"I never had any taste for college, or study, as you know, Mr.
Canfield. It is different with my friend Rodney, who is a Latin
and Greek scholar."

The minister regarded Rodney with new interest.

"Do you think of going to college, Mr. Ropes?" he asked.

"Not at present. I am going back to Montana with Mr. Pettigrew. Perhaps he and I will both go to college next year."

"Excuse me," said Jefferson Pettigrew. "Latin and Greek
ain't in my line. I should make a good deal better miner than
minister."

"It is not desirable that all should become ministers or go to
college," said Mr. Canfield. "I suspect from what I know of
you, Jefferson, that you judge yourself correctly. How long shall
you stay in Burton?"

"I expect to go away tomorrow."

"Your visit is a brief one."

"Yes, I intended to stay longer, but I begin to be homesick after the West."

"Do you expect to make your permanent home there?"

"I can't tell as to that. For the present I can do better there than here."

The conversation lasted for some time. Then Jefferson Pettigrew rose to go.

"Won't you call again, Jefferson?" asked the minister hospitably.

"I shall not have time, but before I go I want to make you a small present," and he put into the hands of the astonished minister four fifty dollar bills.

"Two hundred dollars!" ejaculated the minister. "Why, I heard you only brought home a few hundred."

"I prefer to leave that impression. To you I will say that I am worth a great deal more than that."

"But you mustn't give me so much. I am sure you are too generous for your own interest. Why, it's munificent, princely."

"Don't be troubled about me. I can spare it. Send your boy to college, and next year I will send you another sum equally large."

"How can I thank you, Jefferson?" said Mr. Canfield, the tears coming into his eyes. "Never in forty years have I had such a gift."

"Not even from Squire Sheldon?"

"The squire is not in the habit of bestowing gifts, but he pays a large parish tax. May I—am I at liberty to say from whom I received this liberal donation?"

"Please don't! You can say that you have had a gift from a friend."

"You have made me very happy, Jefferson. Your own conscience will reward you."

Jefferson Pettigrew changed the subject, for it embarrassed him to be thanked.

"That pays me for hard work and privation," he said to Rodney as they walked back to the tavern. "After all there is a great pleasure in making others happy."

"Squire Sheldon hadn't found that out."

"And he never will."

On the way they met the gentleman of whom they had been speaking. He bowed stiffly, for he could not feel cordial to those whom had snatched from him the house for which he had been scheming so long.

"Squire Sheldon," said Jefferson, "you were kind enough to invite Rodney and myself to supper some evening. I am sorry to say that we must decline, as we leave Burton tomorrow."

"Use your own pleasure, Mr. Pettigrew," said the squire coldly.

"It doesn't seem to disappoint the squire very much," remarked Jefferson, laughing, when the great man of the village had passed on.

"It certainly is no disappointment to me."

"Nor to me. The little time I have left I can use more pleasantly than in going to see the squire. I have promised to supper at my uncle's tonight—that is, I have promised for both of us."

Returning to New York, Jefferson and Rodney set about getting ready for their Western journey. Rodney gave some of his wardrobe to Mike Flynn, and bought some plain suits suitable for his new home.

While walking on Broadway the day before the one fixed for his departure he fell in with Jasper Redwood.

"Have you got a place yet, Ropes?" asked Jasper.

"I am not looking for any."

"How is that?" asked Jasper in some surprise.

"I am going to leave the city."

"That is a good idea. All cannot succeed in the city. You may find a chance to work on a farm in the country."

"I didn't say I was going to the country."

"Where are you going, then?"

"To Montana."

"Isn't that a good way off?"

"Yes."

"What are you going to do there?"

"I may go to mining."

"But how can you afford to go so far?"

"Really, Jasper, you show considerable curiosity about my affairs. I have money enough to buy my ticket, and I think I can find work when I get out there."

"It seems to me a crazy idea."

"It might be—for you."

"And why for me?" asked Jasper suspiciously.

"Because you might not be willing to rough it as I am prepared to do."

"I guess you are right. I have always been used to living like a gentleman."

"I hope you will always be able to do so. Now I must bid you good by, as I am busy getting ready for my journey."

Jasper looked after Rodney, not without perplexity.

"I can't make out that boy," he said. "So he is going to be a common miner! Well, that may suit him, but it wouldn't suit me. There is no chance now of his interfering with me, so I am glad he is going to leave the city."

CHAPTER XXIX.

A MINING TOWN IN MONTANA.

The scene changes.

Three weeks later among the miners who were sitting on the narrow veranda of the "Miners' Rest" in Oreville in Montana we recognize two familiar faces and figures—those of Jefferson Pettigrew and Rodney Ropes. Both were roughly clad, and if Jasper could have seen Rodney he would have turned up his nose in scorn, for Rodney had all the look of a common miner.

It was in Oreville that Mr. Pettigrew had a valuable mining property, on which he employed quite a number of men who preferred certain wages to a compensation depending on the fluctuations of fortune. Rodney was among those employed, but although he was well paid he could not get to like the work. Of this, however, he said nothing to Mr. Pettigrew whose company he enjoyed, and whom he held in high esteem.

On the evening in question Jefferson rose from his seat and signed to Rodney to follow him.

"Well, Rodney, how do you like Montana?" he asked.

"Well enough to be glad I came here," answered Rodney.

"Still you are not partial to the work of a miner!"

"I can think of other things I would prefer to do."

"How would you like keeping a hotel?"

"Is there any hotel in search of a manager?" asked Rodney smiling.

"I will explain. Yesterday I bought the 'Miners' Rest.'"

"What—the hotel where we board?"

"Exactly. I found that Mr. Bailey, who has made a comfortable sum of money, wants to leave Montana and go East and I bought the hotel."

"So that hereafter I shall board with you?"

"Not exactly. I propose to put you in charge, and pay you a salary. I can oversee, and give you instructions. How will that suit you?"

"So you think I am competent, Mr. Pettigrew?"

"Yes, I think so. There is a good man cook, and two waiters. The cook will also order supplies and act as steward under you."

"What then will be my duties?"

"You will act as clerk and cashier, and pay the bills. You will have to look after all the details of management. If there is anything you don't understand you will have me to back you up, and advise you. What do you say?"

"That I shall like it much better than mining. My only doubt is as to whether I shall suit you."

"It is true that it takes a smart man to run a hotel, but I think we can do it between us. Now what will you consider a fair salary?"

"I leave that to you, Mr. Pettigrew."

"Then we will call it a hundred and fifty dollars a month and board."

"But, Mr. Pettigrew," said Rodney in surprise, "how can I possibly earn that much?"

"You know we charge big prices, and have about fifty steady boarders. I expect to make considerable money after deducting all the expenses of management."

"My friend Jasper would be very much surprised if he could know the salary I am to receive. In the store I was only paid seven dollars a week."

"The duties were different. Almost any boy could discharge the duties of an entry clerk while it takes peculiar qualities to run a hotel."

"I was certainly very fortunate to fall in with you, Mr. Pettigrew."

"I expect it will turn out fortunate for me too, Rodney."

"When do you want me to start in?"

"Next Monday morning. It is now Thursday evening. Mr. Bailey will turn over the hotel to me on Saturday night. You needn't go to the mines tomorrow, but may remain in the hotel, and he will instruct you in the details of management."

"That will be quite a help to me, and I am at present quite ignorant on the subject."

Rodney looked forward with pleasure to his new employment. He had good executive talent, though thus far he had had no occasion to exercise it. It was with unusual interest that he set about qualifying himself for his new position.

"Young man," said the veteran landlord, "I think you'll do. I thought at first that Jefferson was foolish to put a young boy in my place, but you've got a head on your shoulders, you have! I guess you'll fill the bill."

"I hope to do so, Mr. Bailey."

"Jefferson tells me that you understand Latin and Greek?"

"I know something of them."

"That's what prejudiced me against you. I hired a college boy once as a clerk and he was the worst failure I ever came across. He seemed to have all kinds of sense except common sense. I reckon he was a smart scholar, and he could have made out the bills for the boarders in Latin or Greek if it had been necessary, but he was that soft that any one could cheat him. Things got so mixed up in the department that I had to turn him adrift in a couple of weeks. I surmised you might be the same sort of a chap. If you were it would be a bad lookout for Jefferson."

In Oreville Mr. Pettigrew was so well known that nearly everyone called him by his first name. Mr. Pettigrew did not care for this as he had no false pride or artificial dignity.

"Do you consider this hotel a good property, Mr. Bailey?"

"I'll tell you this much. I started here four years ago, and I've made fifty thousand dollars which I shall take back with me to New Hampshire."

"That certainly is satisfactory."

"I shouldn't wonder if you could improve upon it."

"How does it happen that you sell out such a valuable property, Mr. Bailey? Are you tired of making money?"

"No, but I must tell you that there's a girl waiting for me at home, an old schoolmate, who will become Mrs. Bailey as soon as possible after I get back. If she would come out here I wouldn't sell, but she has a mother that she wouldn't leave, and so I must go to her."

"That is a good reason, Mr. Bailey."

"Besides with fifty thousand dollars I can live as well as I want to in New Hampshire, and hold up my head with the best. You will follow my example some day."

"It will be a long day first, Mr. Bailey, for I am only sixteen."

On Monday morning the old landlord started for his Eastern home and Rodney took his place. It took him some little time to become familiar with all the details of hotel management, but he spared no pains to insure success. He had some trouble at first with the cook who presumed upon his position and Rodney's supposed ignorance to run things as he chose.

Rodney complained to Mr. Pettigrew.

"I think I can fix things, Rodney," he said. "There's a man working for me who used to be cook in a restaurant in New York. I found out about him quietly, for I wanted to be prepared for emergencies. The next time Gordon acts contrary and threatens to leave, tell him he can do as he pleases. Then report to me."

The next day there came another conflict of authority.

"If you don't like the way I manage you can get somebody else," said the cook triumphantly. "Perhaps you'd like to cook the dinner yourself. You're nothing but a boy, and I don't see what Jefferson was thinking of to put you in charge."

"That is his business, Mr. Gordon."

"I advise you not to interfere with me, for I won't stand it."

"Why didn't you talk in this way to Mr. Bailey?"

"That's neither here nor there. He wasn't a boy for one thing."

"Then you propose to have your own way, Mr. Gordon?"

"Yes, I do."

"Very well, then you can leave me at the end of this week."

"What!" exclaimed the cook in profound astonishment. "Are you going crazy?"

"No, I know what I am about."

"Perhaps you intend to cook yourself."

"No, I don't. That would close up the hotel."

"Look here, young feller, you're gettin' too independent! I've a great mind to leave you tonight."

"You can do so if you want to," said Rodney indifferently.

"Then I will!" retorted Gordon angrily, bringing down his fist upon the table in vigorous emphasis.

Oreville was fifty miles from Helena, and that was the nearest point, as he supposed, where a new cook could be obtained.

After supper Rodney told Jefferson Pettigrew what had happened.

"Have I done right?" he asked.

"Yes; we can't have any insubordination here. There can't be two heads of one establishment. Send Gordon to me."

The cook with a defiant look answered the summons.

"I understand you want to leave, Gordon," said Jefferson Pettigrew.

"That depends. I ain't goin' to have no boy dictatin' to me."

"Then you insist upon having your own way without interference."

"Yes, I do."

"Very well, I accept your resignation. Do you wish to wait till the end of the week, or to leave tonight?"

"I want to give it up tonight."

"Very well, go to Rodney and he will pay you what is due you."

"Are you goin' to get along without a cook?" inquired Gordon in surprise.

"No."

"What are you going to do, then?"

"I shall employ Parker in your place."

"What does he know about cookin'?"

"He ran a restaurant in New York for five years, the first part of the time having charge of the cooking. We shan't suffer even if you do leave us."

"I think I will stay," said Gordon in a submissive tone.

"It is too late. You have discharged yourself. You can't stay here on any terms."

Gordon left Oreville the next day a sorely disappointed man, for he had received more liberal pay than he was likely to command elsewhere. The young landlord had triumphed.

CHAPTER XXX.

THE MYSTERIOUS ROBBERY.

At the end of a month Jefferson Pettigrew said: "I've been looking over the books, Rodney, and I find the business is better than I expected. How much did I agree to pay you?"

"A hundred and fifty dollars a month, but if you think that it is too much——"

"Too much? Why I am going to advance you to two hundred and fifty."

"You can't be in earnest, Mr. Pettigrew?"

"I am entirely so."

"That is at the rate of three thousand dollars a year!"

"Yes, but you are earning it."

"You know I am only a boy."

"That doesn't make any difference as long as you understand your business."

"I am very grateful to you, Mr. Pettigrew. My, I can save two hundred dollars a month."

"Do so, and I will find you a paying investment for the money."

"What would Jasper say to my luck?" thought Rodney.

Three months passed without any incident worth recording. One afternoon a tall man wearing a high hat and a Prince

Albert coat with a paste diamond of large size in his shirt bosom entered the public room of the Miners' Rest and walking up to the bar prepared to register his name. As he stood with his pen in his hand Rodney recognized him not without amazement.

It was Louis Wheeler—the railroad thief, whom he had last seen in New York.

As for Wheeler he had not taken any notice of the young clerk, not suspecting that it was an old acquaintance who was familiar with his real character.

"Have you just arrived in Montana, Mr. Wheeler?" asked Rodney quietly.

As Rodney had not had an opportunity to examine his signature in the register Wheeler looked up in quiet surprise.

"Do you know me?" he asked.

"Yes; don't you know me?"

"I'll be blowed if it isn't the kid," ejaculated Wheeler.

"As I run this hotel, I don't care to be called a kid."

"All right, Mr. ——"

"Ropes."

"Mr. Ropes, you are the most extraordinary boy I ever met."

"Am I?"

"Who would have thought of your turning up as a Montana landlord."

"I wouldn't have thought of it myself four months ago. But what brings you out here?"

"Business," answered Wheeler in an important tone.

"Are you going to become a miner?"

"I may buy a mine if I find one to suit me."

"I am glad you seem to be prospering."

"Can you give me a good room?"

"Yes, but I must ask a week's advance payment."

"How much?"

"Twenty five dollars."

"All right. Here's the money."

Louis Wheeler pulled out a well filled wallet and handed over two ten dollar bills and a five.

"Is that satisfactory?" he asked.

"Quite so. You seem better provided with money than when I saw you last."

"True. I was then in temporary difficulty. But I made a good turn in stocks and I am on my feet again."

Rodney did not believe a word of this, but as long as Wheeler was able to pay his board he had no good excuse for refusing him accommodation.

"That rascal here!" exclaimed Jefferson, when Rodney informed him of Wheeler's arrival. "Well, that beats all! What has brought him out here?"

"Business, he says."

"It may be the same kind of business that he had with me. He will bear watching."

"I agree with you, Mr. Pettigrew."

Louis Wheeler laid himself out to be social and agreeable, and made himself quite popular with the other boarders at the hotel. As Jefferson and Rodney said nothing about him, he was taken at his own valuation, and it was reported that he was a heavy capitalist from Chicago who had come to Montana to buy a mine. This theory received confirmation both from his speech and actions.

On the following day he went about in Oreville and examined the mines. He expressed his opinion freely in regard to what he saw, and priced one that was for sale at fifty thousand dollars.

"I like this mine," he said, "but I don't know enough about it to make an offer. If it comes up to my expectations I will try it."

"He must have been robbing a bank," observed Jefferson Pettigrew.

Nothing could exceed the cool assurance with which Wheeler greeted Jefferson and recalled their meeting in New York.

"You misjudged me then, Mr. Pettigrew," he said. "I believe upon my soul you looked upon me as an adventurer—a confidence man."

"You are not far from the truth, Mr. Wheeler," answered Jefferson bluntly.

"Well, I forgive you. Our acquaintance was brief and you judged from superficial impressions."

"Perhaps so, Mr. Wheeler. Have you ever been West before?"

"No."

"When you came to Oreville had you any idea that I was here?"

"No; if I had probably I should not have struck the town, as I knew that you didn't have a favorable opinion of me."

"I can't make out much of that fellow, Rodney," said Jefferson. "I can't understand his object in coming here."

"He says he wants to buy a mine."

"That's all a pretext. He hasn't money enough to buy a mine or a tenth part of it."

"He seems to have money."

"Yes; he may have a few hundred dollars, but mark my words, he hasn't the slightest intention of buying a mine."

"He has some object in view."

"No doubt! What it is is what I want to find out."

There was another way in which Louis Wheeler made himself popular among the miners of Oreville. He had a violin with him, and in the evening he seated himself on the veranda and played popular tunes.

He had only a smattering in the way of musical training, but the airs he played took better than classical music would have done. Even Jefferson Pettigrew enjoyed listening to "Home, Sweet Home" and "The Last Rose of Summer," while the miners were captivated by merry dance tunes, which served to enliven them after a long day's work at the mines.

One day there was a sensation. A man named John O'Donnell came down stairs from his room looking pale and agitated.

"Boys," he said, "I have been robbed."

Instantly all eyes were turned upon him.

"Of what have you been robbed, O'Donnell?" asked Jefferson.

"Of two hundred dollars in gold. I was going to send it home to my wife in Connecticut next week."

"When did you miss it?"

"Just now."

"Where did you keep it?"

"In a box under my bed."

"When do you think it was taken?"

"Last night."

"What makes you think so?"

"I am a sound sleeper, and last night you know was very dark. I awoke with a start, and seemed to hear footsteps. I looked towards the door, and saw a form gliding from the room."

"Why didn't you jump out of bed and seize the intruder whoever he was?"

"Because I was not sure but it was all a dream. I think now it was some thief who had just robbed me."

"I think so too. Could you make out anything of his appearance?"

"I could only see the outlines of his figure. He was a tall man. He must have taken the money from under my bed."

"Did any one know that you had money concealed there?"

"I don't think I ever mentioned it."

"It seems we have a thief among us," said Jefferson, and almost unconsciously his glance rested on Louis Wheeler who was seated near John O'Donnell, "what do you think, Mr. Wheeler?"

"I think you are right, Mr. Pettigrew."

"Have you any suggestion to make?" asked Jefferson. "Have you by chance lost anything?"

"Not that I am aware of."

"Is there any one else here who has been robbed?"

No one spoke.

"You asked me if I had any suggestions to make, Mr. Pettigrew," said Louis Wheeler after a pause. "I have.

"Our worthy friend Mr. O'Donnell has met with a serious loss. I move that we who are his friends make it up to him. Here is my contribution," and he laid a five dollar bill on the table.

It was a happy suggestion and proved popular. Every one present came forward, and tendered his contributions including Jefferson, who put down twenty five dollars.

Mr. Wheeler gathered up the notes and gold and sweeping them to his hat went forward and tendered them to John O'Donnell.

"Take this money, Mr. O'Donnell," he said. "It is the free will offering of your friends. I am sure I may say for them, as for myself, that it gives us all pleasure to help a comrade in trouble."

Louis Wheeler could have done nothing that would have so lifted him in the estimation of the miners.

"And now," he said, "as our friend is out of his trouble I will play you a few tunes on my violin, and will end the day happily."

"I can't make out that fellow, Rodney," said Jefferson when they were alone. "I believe he is the thief, but he has an immense amount of nerve."

CHAPTER XXXI.

MR. WHEELER EXPLAINS.

Probably there was no one at the hotel who suspected Louis Wheeler of being a thief except Rodney and Mr. Pettigrew. His action in starting a contribution for John O'Donnell helped to make him popular. He was establishing a reputation quite new to him, and it was this fact probably that made him less prudent than he would otherwise have been.

As the loss had been made up, the boarders at the Miners' Rest ceased to talk of it. But Jefferson and his young assistant did not forget it.

"I am sure Wheeler is the thief, but I don't know how to bring it home to him," said Jefferson one day, when alone with Rodney.

"You might search him."

"Yes, but what good would that do? It might be found that he had money, but one gold coin is like another and it would be impossible to identify it as the stolen property. If O'Donnell had lost anything else except money it would be different. I wish he would come to my chamber."

"Perhaps he would if he thought you were a sound sleeper."

"That is an idea. I think I can make use of it."

That evening when Wheeler was present Mr. Pettigrew managed to turn the conversation to the subject of sleeping.

"I am a very sound sleeper," he said. "I remember when I was at home sleeping many a time through a severe thunder storm."

"Don't you sometimes wake up in the middle of the night?" asked Rodney.

"Very seldom, if I am in good health."

"It's different with me," said another of the company. "A step on the floor or the opening of the door will wake me up at any time."

"I am glad I am not so easily roused."

"If I had a fish horn," said Rodney, laughing, "I should be tempted to come up in the night and give it a blast before your door."

"That might wake me up," said Mr. Pettigrew. "I wouldn't advise you to try it or the other boarders might get up an indignation meeting."

The same evening Jefferson Pettigrew took out a bag of gold and carelessly displayed it.

"Are you not afraid of being robbed, Mr. Pettigrew?" asked Rodney.

"Oh no. I never was robbed in my life."

"How much money have you there?"

"I don't know exactly. Perhaps six hundred dollars," said Pettigrew in an indifferent tone.

Among those who listened to this conversation with interest was Louis Wheeler. Rodney did not fail to see the covetous gleam of his eyes when the gold was displayed.

The fact was, that Wheeler was getting short of cash and at the time he took John O'Donnell's money—for he was the thief—he had but about twenty dollars left, and of this he contributed five to the relief of the man he had robbed.

His theft realized him two hundred dollars, but this would

not last him long, as the expenses of living at the Miners' Rest were considerable. He was getting tired of Oreville, but wanted to secure some additional money before he left it. The problem was whom to make his second victim.

It would not have occurred to him to rob Jefferson Pettigrew, of whom he stood in wholesome fear, but for the admission that he was an unusually sound sleeper; even then he would have felt uncertain whether it would pay. But the display of the bag of money, and the statement that it contained six hundred dollars in gold proved a tempting bait.

"If I can capture that bag of gold," thought Wheeler, "I shall have enough money to set me up in some new place. There won't be much risk about it, for Pettigrew sleeps like a top. I will venture it."

Jefferson Pettigrew's chamber was on the same floor as his own. It was the third room from No. 17 which Mr. Wheeler occupied.

As a general thing the occupants of the Miners' Rest went to bed early. Mining is a fatiguing business, and those who follow it have little difficulty in dropping off to sleep. The only persons who were not engaged in this business were Louis Wheeler and Rodney Ropes. As a rule the hotel was closed at half past ten and before this all were in bed and sleeping soundly.

When Wheeler went to bed he said to himself, "This will probably be my last night in this tavern. I will go from here to Helena, and if things turn out right I may be able to make my stay there profitable. I shan't dare to stay here long after relieving Pettigrew of his bag of gold."

Unlike Jefferson Pettigrew, Wheeler was a light sleeper. He had done nothing to induce fatigue, and had no difficulty in keeping awake till half past eleven. Then lighting a candle, he examined his watch, and ascertained the time.

"It will be safe enough now," he said to himself.

He rose from his bed, and drew on his trousers. Then in his stocking feet he walked along the corridor till he stood in front of Jefferson Pettigrew's door. He was in doubt as to whether he would not be obliged to pick the lock, but on trying the door he found that it was not fastened. He opened it and stood within the chamber.

Cautiously he glanced at the bed. Mr. Pettigrew appeared to be sleeping soundly.

"It's all right," thought Louis Wheeler. "Now where is the bag of gold?"

It was not in open view, but a little search showed that the owner had put it under the bed.

"He isn't very sharp," thought Wheeler. "He is playing right into my hands. Door unlocked, and bag of gold under the bed. He certainly is a very unsuspicious man. However, that is all the better for me. Really there isn't much credit in stealing where all is made easy for you."

There seemed to be nothing to do but to take the gold from its place of deposit, and carry it back to his own room. While there were a good many lodgers in the hotel, there seemed to be little risk about this, as every one was asleep.

Of course should the bag be found in his room that would betray him, but Mr. Wheeler proposed to empty the gold coins into his gripsack, and throw the bag out of the window into the back yard.

"Well, here goes!" said Wheeler cheerfully, as he lifted the bag, and prepared to leave the chamber. But at this critical moment an unexpected sound struck terror into his soul. It was the sound of a key being turned in the lock.

Nervously Wheeler hastened to the door and tried it. It would not open. Evidently it had been locked from the outside. What could it mean?

At the same time there was a series of knocks on the outside of the door. It was the signal that had been agreed upon between Mr. Pettigrew and Rodney. Jefferson had given his key to Rodney, who had remained up and on the watch for Mr. Wheeler's expected visit. He, too, was in his stocking feet.

As soon as he saw Wheeler enter his friend's chamber he stole up and locked the door on the outside. Then when he heard the thief trying to open the door he rained a shower of knocks on the panel.

Instantly Jefferson Pettigrew sprang out of bed and proceeded to act.

"What are you doing here?" he demanded, seizing Wheeler in his powerful grasp.

"Where am I?" asked Wheeler in a tone of apparent bewilderment.

"Oh, it's you, Mr. Wheeler?" said Jefferson. "Don't you know where you are?"

"Oh, it is my friend, Mr. Pettigrew. Is it possible I am in your room?"

"It is very possible. Now tell me why you are here?"

"I am really ashamed to find myself in this strange position. It is not the first time that I have got into trouble from walking in my sleep."

"Oh, you were walking in your sleep!"

"Yes, friend Pettigrew. It has been a habit of mine since I was a boy. But it seems very strange that I should have been led to your room. How could I get in? Wasn't the door locked?"

"It is locked now?"

"It is strange! I don't understand it," said Wheeler, passing his hand over his forehead.

"Perhaps you understand why you have that bag of gold in your hand."

"Can it be possible?" ejaculated Wheeler in well counterfeited surprise. "I don't know how to account for it."

"I think I can. Rodney, unlock the door and come in."

The key was turned in the lock, and Rodney entered with a lighted candle in his hand.

"You see, Rodney, that I have a late visitor. You will notice also that my bag of gold seems to have had an attraction for him."

"I am ashamed. I don't really know how to explain it except in this way. When you displayed the gold last night it drew my attention and I must have dreamed of it. It was this which drew me unconsciously to your door. It is certainly an interesting fact in mental science."

"It would have been a still more interesting fact if you had carried off the gold."

"I might even have done that in my unconsciousness, but of course I should have discovered it tomorrow morning and would have returned it to you."

"I don't feel by any means sure of that. Look here, Mr. Wheeler, if that is your name, you can't pull the wool over my eyes. You are a thief, neither more nor less."

"How can you misjudge me so, Mr. Pettigrew?"

"Because I know something of your past history. It is clear to me now that you were the person that stole John O'Donnell's money."

"Indeed, Mr. Pettigrew."

"It is useless to protest. How much of it have you left?"

Louis Wheeler was compelled to acknowledge the theft, and returned one hundred dollars to Jefferson Pettigrew.

"Now," said Jefferson, "I advise you to leave the hotel at once. If the boys find out that you are a thief you will stand a chance of being lynched. Get out!"

The next morning Jefferson Pettigrew told the other boarders that Louis Wheeler had had a sudden call East, and it was not for a week that he revealed to them the real reason of Wheeler's departure.

CHAPTER XXXII.

RODNEY FALLS INTO A TRAP.

Rodney had reason to be satisfied with his position as land-lord of the Miners' Rest. His pay was large, and enabled him to put away a good sum every month, but his hours were long and he was too closely confined for a boy of his age. At the end of three months he showed this in his appearance. His good friend Pettigrew saw it, and said one day, "Rodney, you are looking fagged out. You need a change."

"Does that mean that you are going to discharge me?" asked Rodney, with a smile.

"It means that I am going to give you a vacation."

"But what can I do if I take a vacation? I should not like lounging around Oreville with nothing to do."

"Such a vacation would do you no good. I'll tell you the plan I have for you. I own a small mine in Babcock, about fifty miles north of Oreville. I will send you up to examine it, and make a report to me. Can you ride on horseback?"

"Yes."

"That is well, for you will have to make your trip in that way. There are no railroads in that direction, nor any other way of travel except on foot or on horseback. A long ride like that, with hours daily in the open air, will do you good. What do you say to it?"

"I should like nothing better," replied Rodney, with his eyes sparkling. "Only, how will you get along without me?"

"I have a man in my employ at the mines who will do part of your work, and I will have a general oversight of things. So you need not borrow any trouble on that account. Do you think you can find your way?"

"Give me the general direction, and I will guarantee to do so. When shall I start?"

"Day after tomorrow. That will give me one day for making arrangements."

At nine the appointed morning Mr. Pettigrew's own horse stood saddled at the door, and Rodney in traveling costume with a small satchel in his hand, mounted and rode away, waving a smiling farewell to his friend and employer.

Rodney did not hurry, and so consumed two days and a half in reaching Babcock. Here he was cordially received by the superintendent whom Jefferson Pettigrew had placed in charge of the mine. Every facility was afforded him to examine into the management of things and he found all satisfactory.

This part of his journey, therefore, may be passed over. But his return trip was destined to be more exciting.

Riding at an easy jog Rodney had got within fifteen miles of Oreville, when there was an unexpected interruption. Two men started out from the roadside, or rather from one side of the bridle path for there was no road, and advanced to meet him with drawn revolvers.

"Halt there!" one of them exclaimed in a commanding tone.

Rodney drew bridle, and gazed at the two men in surprise.

"What do you want of me?" he asked.

"Dismount instantly!"

"Why should I? What right have you to interfere with my journey?"

"Might gives right," said one of the men sententiously. "It will be best for you to do as we bid you without too much back talk."

"What are you—highwaymen?" asked Rodney.

"You'd better not talk too much. Get off that horse!"

Rodney saw that remonstrance was useless, and obeyed the order.

One of the men seized the horse by the bridle, and led him.

"Walk in front!" he said.

"Where are you going to take me?" asked Rodney.

"You will know in due time."

"I hope you will let me go," urged Rodney, beginning to be uneasy. "I am expected home this evening, or at all events I want to get there."

"No doubt you do, but the Miners' Rest will have to get along without you for a while."

"Do you know me then?"

"Yes; you are the boy clerk at the Miners' Rest."

"You both put up there about two weeks since," said Rodney, examining closely the faces of the two men.

"Right you are, kid!"

"What can you possibly want of me?"

"Don't be too curious. You will know in good time."

Rodney remembered that the two men had remained at the hotel for a day and night. They spent the day in wandering around Oreville.

He had supposed when they came that they were in search of employment, but they had not applied for work and only seemed actuated by curiosity. What could be their object in stopping him now he could not understand.

It would have been natural to suppose they wanted money, but they had not asked for any as yet. He had about fifty dollars in his pocketbook and he would gladly have given them this if it would have insured his release. But not a word had been said about money.

They kept on their journey. Montana is a mountainous State, and they were now in the hilly regions. They kept on for perhaps half an hour, gradually getting upon higher ground, until they reached a precipitous hill composed largely of rock.

Here the two men stopped as if they had reached their journey's end.

One of them advanced to the side of the hill and unlocked a thick wooden door which at first had failed to attract Rodney's attention. The door swung open, revealing a dark passage, cut partly through stone and partly through earth. Inside on the floor was a bell of good size.

One of the men lifted the bell and rang it loudly.

"What does that mean?" thought Rodney, who felt more curious than apprehensive.

He soon learned.

A curious looking negro, stunted in growth, for he was no taller than a boy of ten, came out from the interior and stood at the entrance of the cave, if such it was. His face was large and hideous, there was a hump on his back, and his legs were not a match, one being shorter than the other, so that as he walked, his motion was a curious one. He bent a scrutinizing glance on Rodney.

"Well, Caesar, is dinner ready?" asked one of the men.

"No, massa, not yet."

"Let it be ready then as soon as possible. But first lead the way. We are coming in."

He started ahead, leading the horse, for the entrance was high enough to admit the passage of the animal.

"Push on!" said the other, signing to Rodney to precede him.

Rodney did so, knowing remonstrance to be useless. His

curiosity was excited. He wondered how long the passage was and whither it led.

The way was dark, but here and there in niches was a kerosene lamp that faintly relieved the otherwise intense blackness.

"I have read about such places," thought Rodney, "but I never expected to get into one. The wonder is, that they should bring me here. I can't understand their object."

Rodney followed his guide for perhaps two hundred and fifty feet when they emerged into a large chamber of irregular shape, lighted by four large lamps set on a square wooden table. There were two rude cots in one corner, and it was here apparently that his guides made their home.

There was a large cooking stove in one part of the room, and an appetizing odor showed that Caesar had the dinner under way.

Rodney looked about him in curiosity. He could not decide whether the cave was natural or artificial. Probably it was a natural cave which had been enlarged by the hand of man.

"Now hurry up the dinner, Caesar," said one of the guides. "We are all hungry."

"Yes, massa," responded the obedient black.

Rodney felt hungry also, and hoped that he would have a share of the dinner. Later he trusted to find out the object of his new acquaintances in kidnaping him.

Dinner was soon ready. It was simple, but Rodney thoroughly enjoyed it.

During the meal silence prevailed. After it his new acquaintances produced pipes and began to smoke. They offered Rodney a cigarette, but he declined it.

"I don't smoke," he said.

"Are you a Sunday school kid?" asked one in a sneering tone.

"Well, perhaps so."

"How long have you lived at Oreville?"

"About four months."

"Who is the head of the settlement there?"

"Jefferson Pettigrew."

"He is the moneyed man, is he?"

"Yes."

"Is he a friend of yours?"

"He is my best friend," answered Rodney warmly.

"He thinks a good deal of you, then?"

"I think he does."

"Where have you been—on a journey?"

"Yes, to the town of Babcock."

"Did he send you?"

"Yes."

"What interest has he there?"

"He is chief owner of a mine there."

"Humph! I suppose you would like to know why we brought you here."

"I would very much."

"We propose to hold you for ransom."

"But why should you? I am only a poor boy."

"You are the friend of Jefferson Pettigrew. He is a rich man. If he wants you back he must pay a round sum."

It was all out now! These men were emulating a class of outlaws to be found in large numbers in Italy and Sicily, and were trading upon human sympathy and levying a tax upon human friendship.

CHAPTER XXXIII.

UNDERGROUND.

Rodney realized his position. The alternative was not a pleasant one. Either he must remain in the power of these men, or cost his friend Mr. Pettigrew a large sum as ransom. There was little hope of changing the determination of his captors, but he resolved to try what he could do.

"Mr. Pettigrew is under no obligations to pay money out for me," he said. "I am not related to him, and have not yet known him six months."

"That makes no difference. You are his friend, and he likes you."

"That is the very reason why I should not wish him to lose money on my account."

"Oh, very well! It will be bad for you is he doesn't come to your help."

"Why? What do you propose to do to me?" asked Rodney boldly.

"Better not ask!" was the significant reply.

"But I want to know. I want to realize my position."

"The least that will happen to you is imprisonment in this cave for a term of years."

"I don't think I should like it, but you would get tired of standing guard over me."

"We might, and in that case there is the other thing."

"What other thing?"

"If we get tired of keeping you here, we shall make short work with you."

"Would you murder me?" asked Rodney, horror struck, as he might well be, for death seems terrible to a boy just on the threshold of life.

"We might be obliged to do so."

Rodney looked in the faces of his captors, and he saw nothing to encourage him. They looked like desperate men, who would stick at nothing to carry out their designs.

"I don't see why you should get hold of me," he said. "If you had captured Mr. Pettigrew himself you would stand a better chance of making it pay."

"There is no chance of capturing Pettigrew. If there were we would prefer him to you. A bird in the hand is worth two in the bush."

"How much ransom do you propose to ask?"

This Rodney said, thinking that if it were a thousand dollars he might be able to make it good to his friend Jefferson. But he was destined to be disappointed.

"Five thousand dollars," answered the chief speaker.

"Five thousand dollars!" ejaculated Rodney in dismay. "Five thousand dollars for a boy like me!"

"That is the sum we want."

"If it were one thousand I think you might get it."

"One thousand!" repeated the other scornfully. "That wouldn't half pay us."

"Then suppose you call it two thousand?"

"It won't do."

"Then I suppose I must make up my mind to remain a prisoner."

"Five thousand dollars wouldn't be much to a rich man like Pettigrew. We have inquired, and found out that he is worth at least a hundred thousand dollars. Five thousand is only a twentieth part of this sum."

"You can do as you please, but you had better ask a reasonable amount if you expect to get it."

"We don't want advice. We shall manage things in our own way."

Convinced that further discussion would be unavailing, Rodney relapsed into silence, but now his captors proceeded to unfold their plans.

One of them procured a bottle of ink, some paper and a pen, and set them on the table.

"Come up here, boy, and write to Mr. Pettigrew," he said in a tone of authority.

"What shall I write?"

"Tell him that you are a prisoner, and that you will not be released unless he pays five thousand dollars."

"I don't want to write that. It will be the same as asking him to pay it for me."

"That is what we mean him to understand."

"I won't write it."

Rodney knew his danger, but he looked resolutely into the eyes of the men who held his life in their hands. His voice did not waver, for he was a manly and courageous boy.

"The boy's got grit!" said one of the men to the other.

"Yes, but it won't save him. Boy, are you going to write what I told you?"

"No."

"Are you not afraid that we will kill you?"

"You have power to do it."

"Don't you want to live?"

"Yes. Life is sweet to a boy of sixteen."

"Then why don't you write?"

"Because I think it would be taking a mean advantage of Mr. Pettigrew."

"You are a fool. Roderick, what shall we do with him?"

"Tell him simply to write that he is in our hands."

"Well thought of. Boy, will you do that?"

"Yes."

Rodney gave his consent, for he was anxious that Mr. Pettigrew should know what had prevented him from coming home when he was expected.

"Very well, write! You will know what to say."

Rodney drew the paper to him, and wrote as follows:

DEAR MR. PETTIGREW,

On my way home I was stopped by two men who have confined me in a cave, and won't let me go unless a sum of money is paid for my ransom. I don't know what to do. You will know better than I.

RODNEY ROPES.

His chief captor took the note and read it aloud.

"That will do," he said. "Now he will believe us when we say that you are in our hands."

He signed to Rodney to rise from the table and took his place. Drawing a pile of paper to him, he penned the following note:

Rodney Ropes is in our hands. He wants his liberty and we want money. Send us five thousand dollars, or arrange a meeting at which it can be delivered to us, and he shall go free. Otherwise his death be on your hands.

HIS CAPTORS.

Rodney noticed that this missive was written in a handsome business hand.

"You write a handsome hand," he said.

"I ought to," was the reply. "I was once bookkeeper in a large business house."

"And what—" here Rodney hesitated.

"What made me an outlaw you mean to ask?"

"Yes."

"My nature, I suppose. I wasn't cut out for sober, humdrum life."

"Don't you think you would have been happier?"

"No preaching, kid! I had enough of that when I used to go to church in my old home in Missouri. Here, Caesar!"

"Yes, massa."

"You know Oreville?"

"Yes, massa."

"Go over there and take this letter with you. Ask for Jefferson Pettigrew, and mind you don't tell him where we live. Only if he asks about me and my pal say we are desperate men, have each killed a round dozen of fellows that stood in our way and will stick at nothing."

"All right, massa," said Caesar with an appreciative grin. "How shall I go, massa?"

"You can take the kid's horse. Ride to within a mile of Oreville, then tether the horse where he won't easily be found, and walk over to the mines. Do you understand?"

"Yes, massa."

"He won't probably give you any money, but he may give you a letter. Bring it safely to me."

Caesar nodded and vanished.

For an hour the two men smoked their pipes and chatted. Then they rose, and the elder said: "We are going out, kid, for a couple of hours. Are you afraid to stay alone?"

"Why should I be?"

"That's the way to talk. I won't caution you not to escape, for it would take a smarter lad then you to do it. If you are tired you can lie down on the bed and rest."

"All right!"

"I am sorry we haven't got the morning paper for you to look over," said his captor with a smile. "The carrier didn't leave it this morning."

"I can get along without it. I don't feel much like reading."

"You needn't feel worried. You'll be out of this tomorrow if Jefferson Pettigrew is as much your friend as you think he is."

"The only thing that troubles me is the big price you charge at your hotel."

"Good! The kid has a good wit of his own. After all, we wouldn't mind keeping you with us. It might pay you better than working for Pettigrew."

"I hope you'll excuse my saying it, but I don't like the business."

"You may change your mind. At your age we wouldn't either of us like the sort of life we are leading. Come, John."

The two men went out, but did not allow Rodney to accompany them to the place of exit.

Left to himself, Rodney could think soberly of his plight. He could not foresee whether his captivity would be brief or prolonged.

After a time the spirit of curiosity seized him. He felt tempted to explore the cavern in which he was confined. He took a lamp, and followed in a direction opposite to that taken by his captors.

The cave he found was divided into several irregularly shaped chambers. He walked slowly, holding up the lamp to examine the walls of the cavern. In one passage he stopped short, for something attracted his attention—something the sight of which made his heart beat quicker and filled him with excitement.

CHAPTER XXXIV.

RODNEY'S DISCOVERY.

There was a good reason for Rodney's excitement. The walls of the subterranean passage revealed distinct and rich indications of gold. There was a time, and that not long before, when they would have revealed nothing to Rodney, but since his residence at Oreville he had more than once visited the mines and made himself familiar with surface indications of mineral deposits.

He stopped short and scanned attentively the walls of the passage.

"If I am not mistaken," he said to himself, "this will make one of the richest mines in Montana. But after all what good will it do me? Here am I a prisoner, unable to leave the cave, or communicate with my friends. If Mr. Pettigrew knew what I do he would feel justified in paying the ransom these men want."

Rodney wondered how these rich deposits had failed to attract the attention of his captors, but he soon settled upon the conclusion that they had no knowledge of mines or mining, and were ignorant of the riches that were almost in their grasp.

"Shall I enlighten them?" he asked himself.

It was a question which he could not immediately answer. He resolved to be guided by circumstances.

In order not to excite suspicion he retraced his steps to the apartment used by his captors as a common sitting room—carefully fixing in his mind the location of the gold ore.

We must now follow the messenger who had gone to Oreville with a letter from Rodney's captors.

As instructed, he left his horse, or rather Rodney's, tethered at some distance from the settlement, and proceeded on foot to the Miners' Rest. His strange appearance excited attention and curiosity. Both these feelings would have been magnified had it been known on what errand he came.

"Where can I find Mr. Jefferson Pettigrew?" he asked of a man whom he saw on the veranda.

"At the Griffin Mine," answered the other, removing the pipe from his mouth.

"Where is that?"

"Over yonder. Are you a miner?"

"No. I know nothing about mines."

"Then why do you want to see Jefferson? I thought you might want a chance to work in the mine."

"No; I have other business with him—business of importance," added the black dwarf emphatically.

"If that is the case I'll take you to him. I am always glad to be of service to Jefferson."

"Thank you. He will thank you, too."

The man walked along with a long, swinging gait which made it difficult for Caesar to keep up with him.

"So you have business with Jefferson?" said the man with the pipe, whose curiosity had been excited.

"Yes."

"Of what sort?"

"I will tell him," answered Caesar shortly.

"So it's private, is it?"

"Yes. If he wants to tell you he will."

"That's fair. Well, come along! Am I walking too fast for you?"

"Your legs are much longer than mine."

"That's so. You are a little shrimp. I declare."

A walk of twenty minutes brought them to the Griffin Mine. Jefferson Pettigrew was standing near, giving directions to a party of miners.

"Jefferson," said the man with the pipe, "here's a chap that wants to see you on business of importance. That is, he says it is."

Jefferson Pettigrew wheeled round and looked at Caesar.

"Well," he said, "what is it?"

"I have a letter for you, massa."

"Give it to me."

Jefferson took the letter and cast his eye over it. As he read it his countenance changed and became stern and severe.

"Do you know what is in this letter?" he asked.

"Yes."

"Come with me."

He led Caesar to a place out of earshot.

"What fiend's game is this?" he demanded sternly.

"I can't tell you, massa; I'm not in it."

"Who are those men that have written to me?"

"I don't know their right names. I calls 'em Massa John and Massa Dick."

"It seems they have trapped a boy friend of mine, Rodney Ropes. Did you see him?"

"Yes; I gave him a good dinner."

"That is well. If they should harm a hair of his head I wouldn't rest till I had called them to account. Where have they got the boy concealed?"

"I couldn't tell you, massa."

"You mean, you won't tell me."

"Yes. It would be as much as my life is worth."

"Humph, well! I suppose you must be faithful to your employer. Do you know that these men want me to pay five thousand dollars for the return of the boy?"

"Yes, I heard them talking about it."

"That is a new kind of rascality. Do they expect you to bring back an answer?"

"Yes, massa."

"I must think. What will they do to the boy if I don't give them the money?"

"They might kill him."

"If they do—but I must have time to think the matter over. Are you expected to go back this afternoon?"

"Yes."

"Can you get back? It must be a good distance."

"I can get back."

"Stay here. I will consult some of my friends and see if I can raise the money."

"Very well, massa."

One of those whom Jefferson called into consultation was the person who had guided Caesar to the Griffin Mine.

Quickly the proprietor of the Miners' Rest unfolded the situation.

"Now," he said, "I want two of you to follow this misshapen dwarf, and find out where he comes from. I want to get hold of the scoundrels who sent him to me."

"I will be one," said the man with the pipe.

"Very well, Fred."

"And I will go with Fred," said a long limbed fellow who had been a Kansas cowboy.

"I accept you, Otto. Go armed, and don't lose sight of him."

"Shall you send the money?"

"Not I. I will send a letter that will encourage them to hope for it. I want to gain time."

"Any instructions, Jefferson?"

"Only this, if you see these men, capture or kill them."

"All right."

CHAPTER XXXV.

A BLOODY CONFLICT.

This was the letter that was handed to Caesar:

> I have received your note. I must have time to think,
> and time perhaps to get hold of the gold. Don't harm a
> hair of the boy's head. If so, I will hunt you to death.
>
> JEFFERSON PETTIGREW.
>
> P.S.—Meet me tomorrow morning at the rocky gorge at
> the foot of Black Mountain. Ten o'clock.

Caesar took the letter, and bent his steps in the direction of
the place where he had tethered his horse. He did not observe
that he was followed by two men, who carefully kept him in
sight, without attracting attention to themselves.

When Caesar reached the place where he had tethered the
horse, he was grievously disappointed at not finding him. One
of the miners in roaming about had come upon the animal, and
knowing him to be Jefferson Pettigrew's property, untied him
and rode him back to Oreville.

The dwarf threw up his hands in dismay.

"The horse is gone!" he said in his deep bass voice, "and now

I must walk back, ten long miles, and get a flogging at the end for losing time. It's hard luck," he groaned.

The loss was fortunate for Fred and Otto who would otherwise have found it hard to keep up with the dwarf.

Caesar breathed a deep sigh, and then started on his wearisome journey. Had the ground been even it would have troubled him less, but there was a steep upward grade, and his short legs were soon weary. Not so with his pursuers, both of whom were long limbed and athletic.

We will go back now to the cave and the captors of Rodney. They waited long and impatiently for the return of their messenger. Having no knowledge of the loss of the horse, they could not understand what detained Caesar.

"Do you think the rascal has played us false?" said Roderick.

"He would be afraid to."

"This man Pettigrew might try to bribe him. It would be cheaper than to pay five thousand dollars."

"He wouldn't dare. He knows what would happen to him," said John grimly.

"Then why should he be so long?"

"That I can't tell."

"Suppose we go out to meet him. I begin to feel anxious lest we have trusted him too far."

"I am with you!"

The two outlaws took the path which led to Oreville, and walked two miles before they discovered Caesar coming towards them at a slow and melancholy gait.

"There he is, and on foot! What does it mean?"

"He will tell us."

"Here now, you black imp! where is the horse?" demanded Roderick.

"I done lost him, massa."

"Lost him? You'll get a flogging for this, unless you bring good news. Did you see Jefferson Pettigrew?"

"Yes, massa."

"Did he give you any money?"

"No; he gave me this letter."

Roderick snatched it from his hand, and showed it to John.

"It seems satisfactory," he said. "Now how did you lose the horse?"

Caesar told him.

"You didn't fasten him tight."

"Beg your pardon, massa, but I took good care of that."

"Well, he's gone; was probably stolen. That is unfortunate; however you may not have been to blame."

Luckily for Caesar the letter which he brought was considered satisfactory, and this palliated his fault in losing the horse.

The country was so uneven that the two outlaws did not observe that they were followed, until they came to the entrance of the cave. Then, before opening the door, John looked round and caught sight of Fred and Otto eying them from a little distance.

He instantly took alarm.

"Look," he said, "we are followed. Look behind you!"

His brother turned and came to the same conclusion.

"Caesar," said Roderick, "did you ever see those men before?"

"No, massa."

"They must have followed you from Oreville. Hello, you two!" he added striding towards the miners. "What do you want here?"

Fred and Otto had accomplished their object in ascertaining the place where Rodney was confined, and no longer cared for concealment.

"None of your business!" retorted Fred independently. "The place is as free to us as to you."

"Are you spies?"

"I don't intend to answer any of your questions."

"Clear out of here!" commanded Roderick in a tone of authority.

"Suppose we don't?"

Roderick was a man of quick temper, and had never been in the habit of curbing it. He was provoked by the independent tone of the speaker, and without pausing to think of the imprudence of his actions, he raised his rifle and pointing at Fred shot him in the left arm.

The two miners were both armed, and were not slow in accepting the challenge. Simultaneously they raised their rifles and fired at the two men. The result was that both fell seriously wounded and Caesar set up a howl of dismay, not so much for his masters as from alarm for himself.

Fred and Otto came forward, and stood looking down upon the outlaws, who were in the agonies of death.

"It was our lives or theirs," said Fred coolly, for he had been long enough in Montana to become used to scenes of bloodshed.

"Yes," answered Otto. "I think these two men are the notorious Dixon brothers who are credited with a large number of murders. The country will be well rid of them."

Roderick turned his glazing eyes upon the tall miner. "I wish I had killed you," he muttered.

"No doubt you do. It wouldn't have been your first murder."

"Don't kill me, massa!" pleaded Caesar in tones of piteous entreaty.

"I don't know," answered Fred. "That depends on yourself. If you obey us strictly we will spare you."

"Try me, massa!"

"You black hound!" said Roderick hoarsely. "If I were not disabled I'd kill you myself."

Here was a new danger for poor Caesar, for he knew Roderick's fierce temper.

"Don't let him kill me!" he exclaimed, affrighted.

"He shall do you no harm. Will you obey me?"

"Tell me what you want, massa."

"Is the boy these men captured inside?"

"Yes, massa."

"Open the cave, then. We want him."

"Don't do it," said Roderick, but Caesar saw at a glance that his old master, of whom he stood in wholesome fear, was unable to harm him, and he proceeded to unlock the door.

"Go and call the boy!" said Fred.

Caesar disappeared within the cavern, and soon emerged with Rodney following him.

"Are you unhurt?" asked Fred anxiously.

"Yes, and overjoyed to see you. How came you here?"

"We followed the nigger from Oreville."

What happened afterwards Rodney did not need to inquire, for the two outstretched figures, stiffening in death, revealed it to him.

"They are the Dixon brothers, are they not?" asked Fred, turning to Caesar.

"Yes, massa."

"Then we are entitled to a thousand dollars each for their capture. I have never before shed blood, but I don't regret ending the career of these scoundrels."

Half an hour later the two outlaws were dead and Rodney and his friends were on their way back to Oreville.

Rodney was received by Jefferson Pettigrew with open arms.

"Welcome home, boy!" he said. "I was very much worried about you."

"I was rather uneasy about myself," returned Rodney.

"Well, it's all over, and all's well that ends well. You are free and there has been no money paid out. Fred and Otto have done a good thing in ridding the world of the notorious Dixon brothers. They will be well paid, for I understand there is a standing reward of one thousand dollars for each of them dead or alive. I don't know but you ought to have a share of this, for it was through you that the outlaws were trapped."

"No, Mr. Pettigrew, they are welcome to the reward. If I am not mistaken I shall make a good deal more out of it than they."

"What do you mean?"

Upon this Rodney told the story of what he had seen in the cavern.

"When I said I, I meant we, Mr. Pettigrew. I think if the gold there is as plentiful as I think it is we shall do well to commence working it."

"It is yours, Rodney, by right of first discovery."

"I prefer that you should share it with me."

"We will go over tomorrow and make an examination. Was there any one else who seemed to have a claim to the cave except the Dixons?"

"No. The negro, Caesar, will still be there, perhaps."

"We can easily get rid of him."

The next day the two friends went over to the cavern. Caesar was still there, but he had an unsettled, restless look, and seemed undecided what to do.

"What are you going to do, Caesar?" asked Pettigrew. "Are you going to stay here?"

"I don't know, massa. I don't want to lib here. I'm afraid I'll see the ghostes of my old massas. But I haven't got no money."

"If you had money where would you go?"

"I'd go to Chicago. I used to be a whitewasher, and I reckon I'd get work at my old trade."

"That's where you are sensible, Caesar. This is no place for you. Now I'll tell you what I'll do. I'll give you a hundred dollars, and you can go where you like. But I shall want you to go away at once."

"I'll go right off, massa," said Caesar, overjoyed. "I don't want to come here no more."

"Have you got anything belonging to you in the cave?"

"No, massa, only a little kit of clothes."

"Take them and go."

In fifteen minutes Caesar had bidden farewell to his home, and Rodney and Jefferson were left in sole possession of the cavern.

"Now, Mr. Pettigrew, come and let me show you what I saw. I hope I have made no mistake."

Rodney led the way to the narrow passage already described.

By the light of a lantern Mr. Pettigrew examined the walls. For five minutes not a word was said.

"Well, what do you think of it?" asked Rodney anxiously.

"Only this: that you have hit upon the richest gold deposits in Montana. Here is a mining prospect that will make us both rich."

"I am glad I was not mistaken," said Rodney simply.

"Your capture by the Dixon brothers will prove to have been the luckiest event in your life. I shall lose no time in taking possession in our joint name."

There was great excitement when the discovery of the gold deposits was made known. In connection with the killing of the outlaws, it was noised far and wide. The consequence was that there was an influx of mining men, and within a week Rodney and Jefferson were offered a hundred thousand dollars for a half interest in the mine by a Chicago syndicate.

"Say a hundred and fifty thousand, and we accept the offer," said Jefferson Pettigrew.

After a little haggling this offer was accepted, and Rodney found himself the possessor of seventy five thousand dollars in cash.

"It was fortunate for me when I fell in with you, Mr. Pettigrew," he said.

"And no less fortunate for me, Rodney. This mine will bring us in a rich sum for our share, besides the cash we already have in hand."

"If you don't object, Mr. Pettigrew, I should like to go to New York and continue my education. You can look after my interests here, and I shall be willing to pay you anything you like for doing so."

"There won't be any trouble about that, Rodney. I don't blame you for wanting to obtain an education. It isn't in my line. You can come out once a year, and see what progress we are making. The mine will be called the Rodney Mine after you."

The Miners' Rest was sold to the steward, as Mr. Pettigrew was too busy to attend to it, and in a week Rodney was on his way to New York.

CHAPTER XXXVII.

CONCLUSION.

Otis Goodnow arrived at his place of business a little earlier than usual, and set himself to looking over his mail. Among other letters was one written on paper bearing the name of the Fifth Avenue Hotel. He came to this after a time and read it.

It ran thus:

DEAR SIR:

I was once in your employ, though you may not remember my name. I was in the department of Mr. Redwood, and there I became acquainted with Jasper Redwood, his nephew. I was discharged, it is needless to recall why. I had saved nothing, and of course I was greatly embarrassed. I could not readily obtain another place, and in order to secure money to pay living expenses I entered into an arrangement with Jasper Redwood to sell me articles, putting in more than I paid for. These I was enabled to sell at a profit to smaller stores. This was not as profitable as it might have been to me, as I was obliged to pay Jasper a commission for his agency. Well, after a time it was ascertained that articles were missing, and search was made for the thief. Through a cunningly devised scheme of Jasper's the theft was ascribed to Rodney Ropes, a younger clerk, and he was discharged. Ropes was a fine young fellow, and I have always been sorry that he got into trouble through our agency, but there seeemed no help for it. It must rest on him or us. He protested his innocence, but was not believed. I wish to say now that he was absolutely innocent, and only Jasper and myself were to blame. If you doubt my statement I will call today, and you may confront me with Jasper. I desire that justice should be done.

PHILIP CARTON.

"Call Mr. Redwood," said the merchant, summoning a boy.

In five minutes Mr. Redwood entered the office of his employer.

"You sent for me, sir?"

"Yes, Mr. Redwood; cast your eye over this letter."

James Redwood read the letter, and his face showed the agitation he felt.

"I don't know anything about this, Mr. Goodnow," he said at last.

"It ought to be inquired into."

"I agree with you. If my nephew is guilty I want to know it."

"We will wait till the writer of this letter calls. Do you remember him?"

"Yes, sir; he was discharged for intemperance."

At twelve o'clock Philip Carton made his appearance, and asked to be conducted to Mr. Goodnow's private office.

"You are the writer of this letter?" asked the merchant.

"Yes sir."

"And you stand by the statements it contains?"

"Yes, sir."

"Why, at this late day, have you made a confession?"

"Because I wish to do justice to Rodney Ropes, who has been unjustly accused, and also because I have been meanly treated by Jasper Redwood, who has thrown me over now that he has no further use for me."

"Are you willing to repeat your statements before him?"

"I wish to do so."

"Call Jasper Redwood, Sherman," said the merchant, addressing himself to Sherman White, a boy recently taken into his employ.

Jasper entered the office, rather surprised at the summons. When he saw his accomplice, he changed color, and looked confused.

"Jasper," said the merchant, "read this letter and tell me what you have to say in reply."

Jasper ran his eye over the letter, while his color came and went.

"Well?"

"It's a lie," said Jasper hoarsely.

"Do you still insist that the articles taken from my stock were taken by Rodney Ropes?"

"Yes, sir."

"What do you say, Mr. Carton?"

"Not one was taken by Rodney Ropes. Jasper and I are responsible for them all."

"What proof can you bring?"

"Mr. James Redwood will recall the purchase I made at the time of the thefts. He will recall that I always purchased of Jasper."

"That is true," said Mr. Redwood in a troubled voice.

"Do you confess, Jasper Redwood?"

"No, sir."

"If you will tell the truth, I will see that no harm comes to you. I want to clear this matter up."

Jasper thought the matter over. He saw that the game was up—and decided rapidly that confession was the best policy.

"Very well, sir, if I must I will do so, but that man put me up to it."

"You did not need any putting up to it. I wish young Ropes were here, that I might clear him."

As if in answer to the wish a bronzed and manly figure appeared at the office door. It was Rodney, but taller and more robust than when he left the store nearly a year before.

"Rodney Ropes!" ejaculated Jasper in great surprise.

"Yes, Jasper, I came here to see you, and beg you to free me from the false charge which was brought against me when I was discharged from this store. I didn't find you in your usual places, and was directed here."

"Ropes," said Mr. Goodnow, "your innocence has been established. This man," indicating Philip Carton, "has confessed that it was he and Jasper who stole the missing articles."

"I am thankful that my character has been cleared."

"I am ready to take you back into my employ."

"Thank you, sir, but I have now no need of a position. I shall be glad if you will retain Jasper."

"You are very generous to one who has done so much to injure you."

"Indirectly he put me in the way of making a fortune. If you will retain him, Mr. Goodnow, I will guarantee to make up any losses you may incur from him."

"How is this? Are you able to make this guarantee?"

"I am worth seventy five thousand dollars in money, besides being owner of a large mining property in Montana."

"This is truly wonderful! And you have accumulated all this since you left my store?"

"Yes, sir."

"Rodney," said Jasper, going up to his old rival, and offering his hand. "I am sorry I tried to injure you. It was to save myself, but I see now how meanly I acted."

"That speech has saved you," said the merchant. "Go back to your work. I will give you another chance."

"Will you take me back also, Mr. Goodnow?" asked Philip Carton.

The merchant hesitated.

"No, Mr. Carton," said Rodney. "I will look out for you. I will send you to Montana with a letter to my partner. You can do better there than here."

Tears came into the eyes of the ex-clerk.

"Thank you," he said gratefully. "I should prefer it. I will promise to turn over a new leaf; and justify your recommendation."

"Come to see me this evening at the Fifth Avenue Hotel, and I will arrange matters."

"Shall you stay in the city long, Ropes?" asked the merchant.

"About a week."

"Come and dine with me on Tuesday evening."

"Thank you, sir."

Later in the day Rodney sought out his old room mate Mike Flynn. He found Mike in a bad case. He had a bad cold, but did not dare to give up work, because he wouldn't be able to meet his bills. He was still in the employ of the District Telegraph Company.

"Give the company notice, Mike," said Rodney. "Henceforth I will take care of you. You can look upon me as your rich uncle," he added with a smile.

"I will be your servant, Rodney."

"Not a bit of it. You will be my friend. But you must obey me implicitly. I am going to send you to school, and give you a chance to learn something. Next week I shall return to Dr. Sampson's boarding school and you will go with me as my friend and room mate."

"But, Rodney, you will be ashamed of me. I am awfully shabby."

"You won't be long. You shall be as well dressed as I am."

A week later the two boys reached the school. It would have been hard for any of Mike's old friends to recognize him in the handsomely dressed boy who accompanied Rodney.

"Really, Mike, you are quite good looking, now that you are well dressed," said Rodney.

"Oh, go away with you, Rodney? It's fooling me you are!"

"Not a bit of it. Now I want you to improve your time and learn as fast as you can."

"I will, Rodney."

A year later Rodney left school, but he kept Mike there two years longer. There had been a great change in the telegraph boy, who was quick to learn. He expects, when he leaves school, to join Rodney in Montana.

I will not attempt to estimate Rodney's present wealth, but he is already prominent in financial circles in his adopted State. Philip Carton is prospering, and is respected by his new friends, who know nothing of his earlier life.

As I write, Rodney has received a letter from his old guardian, Benjamin Fielding. The letter came from Montreal.

"My dear Rodney," he wrote. "I have worked hard to redeem the past, and restore to you your fortune. I have just succeeded, and send you the amount with interest. It leaves me little or nothing, but my mind is relieved. I hope you have not had to suffer severely from my criminal carelessness, and that you will live long to enjoy what rightfully belongs to you."

In reply Rodney wrote: "Please draw on me for fifty thousand dollars. I do not need it, and you do. Five years from now, if you can spare the money you may send it to me. Till then use it without interest. I am worth much more than the sum my father intrusted to you for me."

This offer was gratefully accepted, and Mr. Fielding is now in New York, where he is likely to experience a return of his former prosperity.

As for Rodney, his trials are over. They made a man of him, and proved a blessing in disguise.

5361